BROMLEY GIRLS

Martha Mendelsohn

BROMLEY GIRLS

Texas Tech University Press

This book is typeset in Century Schoolbook. The paper used in this book meets the minimum requirements of ANSI/NISO Z39.48-1992 (R1997). ∞

Designed by Kasey McBeath

Library of Congress Cataloging-in-Publication Data
Mendelsohn, Martha.
    Bromley girls / Martha Mendelsohn.
        pages cm
    Summary: After Emily Winter, fourteen, makes a promising start at a posh, academically-challenging Manhattan girls' school in 1955, things turn sour but she discovers a knack for leadership as she copes with her best friend Phoebe's snubs, a newborn brother, snobbish classmates, and more.
    ISBN 978-0-89672-922-3 (paperback) — ISBN 978-0-89672-923-0 (e-book) [1. Friendship—Fiction. 2. Schools—Fiction. 3. Antisemitism—Fiction. 4. Prejudices—Fiction. 5. Eating disorders—Fiction. 6. Conduct of life—Fiction. 7. New York (N.Y—History—1951—Fiction.] I. Title.
        PZ7.1.M47Bro 2015
        [Fic]—dc23   2014044593

15 16 17 18 19 20 21 22 23 / 9 8 7 6 5 4 3 2 1

Texas Tech University Press
Box 41037 | Lubbock, Texas 79409-1037 USA
800.832.4042 | ttup@ttu.edu | www.ttupress.org

For Fred

CONTENTS

ACKNOWLEDGMENTS

No end of gratitude to Elaine Edelman, Jessamyn Hope, Rosanne Ehrlich, Elizabeth Albrecht, Lindsley Borsodi, Nina Mishkin, and the other gifted members—past and present—of my Sarah Lawrence alumnae writing group. Much appreciation to Thane Rosenbaum, whose support went beyond the call of friendship. I'm also very grateful to Karen Clark, Joanna Conrad, Jada Rankin, and Amanda Werts at TTUP; and to copyeditor extraordinaire Dawn Ollila. A special shout-out to Alison Pollet, whose wonderful novel *Nobody Was Here* led me to try my hand at young adult fiction, and to my former classmate and everlasting friend Lisa Null, for her revelatory e-mails. Immeasurable thanks to early encouraging readers Fred, James, Nathaniel, Richard, and their spouses Carrie and Damla; to my sister Janie; to the many readers and writers in my family—Jane, Nick, Gracie, Sasha, and Lily (a highly discerning young adult)—and to my mother, Dorothy Neustadter, whose passion for books inspired my own.

BROMLEY GIRLS

1 ❀ Uniforms

Masters in this hall,
Hear ye news today-ay-ay
Brought from over-seas
And ever you I pray . . .

"Why do we sing about masters?" Emily Winter asked as she and Phoebe Barrett lined up with the other ninth graders and stomped into the assembly hall. Soprano and alto voices soared in near-perfect unison as Mr. Carslake, the music teacher, pounded out a string of thundering chords. "Bromley is an all-girls school, isn't it?"

It was what their teacher, Miss Lockwood, would call a rhetorical question. Everybody knew that Mr. Carslake was the only male on the premises, even though the school had been founded ninety-nine years earlier by a man, renowned encyclopedia editor Professor Archibald Q. Bromley, to give his friends' daughters almost as rigorous an education as their sons.

"'Masters in This Hall' is a Bromley favorite," Cressida Whitcroft hissed, spinning around from her seat in the row ahead. She twirled the blond, S-shaped dip grazing her right eyebrow. "I guess you sang other songs at your old school."

She was right. "Rudolph the Red-Nosed Reindeer" was the only Christmas song Emily had sung at Great Woods Junior High. Last summer her mother and father, Lenore and Sidney

Winter, had moved from Long Island to Manhattan with her—their only child, though not for long. After fourteen years with just Emily, her mother was having a baby.

In Great Woods, most everyone was Jewish. Phoebe belonged to the Fifth Avenue Episcopal Church.

Emily and Phoebe had become instant friends on the first day of school before another assembly, laughing about James Dean. Not ha-ha laughing, exactly. There was nothing funny about how America's number one heartthrob had been killed speeding in his Porsche the week before. The girls dissolving in weeping fits as if they'd lost the love of their lives—they made Emily and Phoebe laugh.

Phoebe had pointed to Cressida, in the middle of a group of tearful girls. She wore a black velvet headband tucked into her perfectly turned under pageboy, and her figure had a shape even in the baggy Bromley uniform. "She's not only beautiful and athletic, she gets straight Veegees, too," Phoebe said. Veegee was what everyone called Very Good, the next-to-highest grade. The highest grade was Distinguished, which only five girls had ever gotten in the history of the school. "I wouldn't touch her with a ten-foot pole. She's conceited and cold as ice unless she approves of you and, to be perfectly frank, that's unlikely."

Emily had to agree. Cressida types steered clear of girls like her, with thick glasses and frizzy hair. Not that Emily hadn't tried to latch on to girls like Cressida in Great Woods; her best friend, Melissa, had dressed in all the latest clothes and was often aloof, but other times she seemed to want to be with Emily morning, noon, and night. Emily had tagged behind Melissa—literally. Melissa would walk fast and Emily would try to catch up. And Emily had tried to keep up with Melissa in other ways—she was so poised and self-confident.

Now she would probably tag behind Phoebe.

She followed her up seven flights of stairs, two steps at a

time, to the bookstore to buy her English, algebra, French, history, Latin and biology textbooks, and to stock up on the custom-made 3 × 5 notebooks—the same size as examination blue books—which Bromley girls used instead of regular loose-leaf folders.

"I have a confession to make," Phoebe said breathlessly. "I'm probably the only girl in the class who didn't have a crush on James Dean.

"I didn't either!" Emily said. She had always found him too moody looking.

"His lips are too pouty," Phoebe said. She crinkled her snub nose in disapproval. "I mean, *were*."

"His eyes were too squinty," said Emily.

"I still want to see *Rebel Without a Cause,* though," Phoebe said. It was the actor's next-to-last movie, and it was coming to the Trans-Lux Eighty-fifth Street in a few days. Everybody wanted to see it.

"Me too!" Emily said. She wasn't just following Phoebe, she told herself. She actually agreed with her. Much of the time she'd only pretended to agree with Melissa. Especially about James Dean. Melissa had been madly in love with him, and Emily had put on a good act of worshipping him, too. Did she have more in common with Phoebe?

Still breathless, they ran down a flight to the ninth-grade homeroom, carrying their heavy books. Would Emily have to climb up and down six flights every day? That morning a woman in a maid's prim black uniform with a ruffled apron had ushered her into the school vestiary. Maids but no elevator? It didn't make sense.

And in the long hallway outside the homeroom there were no free lockers. "I forgot. Ninth grade often has at least one extra girl," Phoebe said. "That's because some people will be leaving for boarding school next year. You can share my locker for now."

As she stuffed her books on top of Phoebe's, Emily had another thought. Maybe Bromley hadn't expected her after all.

Maybe her mother had forgotten to fill out the necessary enrollment forms because she was too busy being pregnant.

Her mother didn't seem to mind that she was thirty-five and probably the oldest pregnant woman in New York City.

Because of all the girls crying their eyes out, Miss Eunice Foxworthy, Bromley's headmistress, had replaced the usual opening assembly, in which students read their "My Summer Experience" papers, with an assembly on Coping with Tragedy and Its Aftermath.

Echoing the expressions on the masks of Comedy and Tragedy etched into the wall on either side of the assembly hall stage, Miss Foxworthy smiled fleetingly, then frowned, as she mounted the steps to the podium.

"We gather to pay our respects to James Byron Dean, a gifted interpreter of the dramatic arts, who met with a tragic, untimely end," Miss Foxworthy said solemnly. "In the words of the inimitable William Shakespeare, 'Cowards die many times before their deaths; the valiant never taste of death but once.' Be strong, Bromley girls, and when you learn to drive a motor vehicle, observe the speed limit."

To allow the students to grieve properly, school was dismissed early.

"Where do you live?" Phoebe asked, as they pushed through Bromley's massive front door.

"1163 Park Avenue—between Ninety-third and Ninety-fourth," Emily said.

"The building that looks like a castle?"

"That's the one." There were grand apartment buildings with uniformed doormen and sleek awnings all along Park Avenue, but, with turrets and buttresses and a driveway that looked like a moat, Emily's apartment building was unique.

"We'll take the Crosstown together," Phoebe said.

Emily watched carefully as the bus jolted past Second Avenue, then Third, then Lexington. She was still trying to get the city's streets straight.

"It must be great to live so near the Metropolitan Museum.

I'm miles away on the West Side. Do you ever visit the knights in shining armor?"

"Knights?" Emily was obsessed with knights and ladies and the Age of Chivalry. She'd read up on the romance of Lancelot and Guinevere, and Tristan and Isolde and the fatal love potion. She'd even started referring to her parents as "Lady Lenore" and "Lord Sidney." But she hadn't been to the Metropolitan yet.

"Scads of them!" Phoebe said, with a smile that carved deep dimples in her cheeks. "In the Arms and Armor Room. Not actual knights, of course. After so many centuries, they'd be decomposed. Just their suits of armor. You have to imagine the knights inside them."

"Of course," Emily said. Something else in common!

Phoebe opened her book bag and pulled out *The Canterbury Tales*. "To think that we're actually studying the Middle Ages this year! It's my favorite historical period."

"Mine, too!" Emily said.

"I wish I'd been born in the twelfth century."

"Me, too." But Emily wasn't so sure. She suspected it was more fun, or at least more comfortable, to live in the twentieth century. But the Middle Ages were more interesting—she didn't have to pretend to agree on that.

"I hate Current Events, don't you? Everything about the Cold War is so incredibly dreary."

It was more scary than dreary, Emily thought. What if Russia decided to drop the hydrogen bomb? Once again, she agreed. She shouldn't disagree with a brand-new friend quite yet, she told herself.

"Can you go see the knights with me this Saturday?" Phoebe asked.

"Yes, I think so," Emily said. She had no other plans, but maybe it was best not to sound too eager.

"Don't tell a soul, but I'm madly in love with a knight," Phoebe said.

"Which one?" Emily asked. Was it Sir Lancelot? Or maybe Tristan. Emily had crushes on medieval heroes, too.

"On the actor Laurence Olivier, that's who. Queen Elizabeth dubbed him—that's why he's called *Sir* Laurence Olivier," Phoebe said.

"No kidding! I have a crush on him, too." Emily had seen *Wuthering Heights* three times because Laurence Olivier played Heathcliff. But he wasn't exactly the teen idol of the moment. She had never told Melissa about her infatuation.

Now she pictured him as a knight jousting for the honor of his lady fair, who would of course be his wife, Vivien Leigh. His soulful brown eyes and the deep cleft in his chin would be partly obscured by his visor. He would topple his opponent with a swipe of the lance while Lady Vivien looked on, green eyes flashing.

"Between you, me, and the lamppost, I think he's the biggest dreamboat of all. I call him L.O., the first letters of the word love," Phoebe said.

From then on, Emily would, too. But she was fickle. She was always falling in love. Before Laurence Olivier, she'd had crushes on the television cowboys Gene Autry and Roy Rogers, who strummed their guitars on horseback. Before them, there was Howdy Doody, even though he was a marionette. She'd had a crush on him, too.

"While we're on the subject of the opposite sex, better start thinking about calling a boy to invite to the class dance in January," Phoebe said.

Call a boy? To invite to a dance? In Great Woods no girl would be caught dead calling up a boy unless he was a partner on the debating team, or a cousin, or someone you'd known your whole life—like Emily's neighbor Davy Hirsch, who was the only boy Emily could possibly invite.

"But it's only September!" Emily objected.

"Aren't you starting dancing school soon?" Phoebe said.

"Of course. My first class at Flora Freund's is next Friday." In Great Woods only a few kids went to dancing school, and people made fun of them. But Great Woods High was coed. At first Emily had refused to go to Flora Freund's, but Lady Lenore insisted that dancing school was the only way for students from all-girls and all-boys schools to meet.

A long pause followed. "I go to Miss Thornberry's," Phoebe said. "Like most of the girls at Bromley."

Was there something wrong with Flora Freund's? Emily wondered. Why hadn't her mother thought of Miss Thornberry's?

"Look, when the time comes, I'll help you write a script for the phone call," Phoebe said, as if reading her mind. "That way nothing will be left to chance."

Even if she and Phoebe would be going to different dancing schools, Emily couldn't believe how lucky she was to have found a friend like Phoebe. A girl who was so willing to help. A friend who was as crazy about the Middle Ages and Laurence Olivier as she was. Secretly she'd been afraid all the girls at Bromley would be like that Cressida. But maybe she shouldn't congratulate herself just yet. What about Cressida's friends, the James Dean mourners, the ones who hadn't even said hello?

The bus snorted to a stop on Park Avenue. "Stay on till Madison," Phoebe urged, tugging at Emily's uniform skirt. "You can take the No. 4 bus like I do and get off at 94th Street." The No. 4 crossed Central Park at 110th Street, she explained, and continued all the way west to her apartment building on Claremont Avenue near Columbia University, where her father had once been a professor of natural sciences. "No one else in our class lives in my neighborhood," she said gloomily.

Emily's mother had warned her about the West Side. It wasn't safe, especially along the seedy side streets. Drunks and dope fiends and lots of poor people lived there.

It didn't take Emily long to figure out that Bromley was assembly crazy. Coping with Tragedy and Its Aftermath was followed by the rescheduled My Summer Experience assembly, which was followed by the United Nations Day, Founder's Day, and Thanksgiving assemblies—and by the Sixtieth Day of School assembly, in which lower schoolers had to think up different ways of adding up to sixty.

And now, before winter vacation, the Christmas assembly.

"Get a load of Old Foxy!" Emily whispered. Miss Foxworthy tripped on the hem of her billowing black robe as she waddled up the steps to the podium.

She cleared her throat three times. "And it came to pass in those days that there went out a decree from Caesar Augustus," she read from the story of Jesus Christ's birth.

"Humility and meekness—these are the values expounded in the Gospels," she continued, hunching over the lectern. "Those of us born into privilege would do well to embrace them. Remember that you still represent the school when you are on vacation. Even out of uniform, schussing down the Alps or sunbathing on the Riviera, avoid ostentation and be courteous. Dress and act appropriately! Comport yourself like Bromley girls!"

A thought popped into Emily's head. Had Old Foxy ever had a posture picture taken?

Before the first gym period, Emily and Phoebe had stripped to their underwear and pulled butterfly robes over their heads to parade single file with the rest of the class while Miss Stillman, the head of the gym department, snapped full-body photographs from the front, side, and rear. The pictures were supposed to show if anyone had curvature of the spine.

"Christmas is come in and no folk shall be sad," Emily and Phoebe sang as they marched past Professor Bromley's scowling portrait. Vacation had officially begun.

In 7G, the ninth-grade homeroom, the girls threw camel hair coats over their charcoal gray uniforms. They tossed gray book bags over their shoulders and wound six-foot-long striped, woolen college scarves around their necks. Phoebe's and Cressida's were blue and white, the colors of Yale, their fathers' alma mater. For some reason, no one wore scarves from any of the women's colleges Bromley graduates attended. As soon as Emily had noticed Phoebe and the other girls wearing those striped scarves when the weather turned colder, she'd knew she'd had to have one, too. Hers was orange and black. It had arrived in the mail the day before.

"So your father went to Princeton?" Cressida said.

"Not really." Emily was not about to tell Cressida that her father had gone to night school or worked in her grandfather's stationery store before inventing Whirlex, a circular card file that had just won the Desktop Office Appliance of the Year award.

It was her father who suggested Emily get her scarf from Princeton. "Orange and black go with your coloring, Twizzle," he said. He called her Twizzle because her wavy black hair reminded him of licorice candy. He helped her write to the Princeton bookstore, and they ordered the scarf and some orange-and-black-striped book covers and a pennant, too.

"See you in 1956!" The girls shouted to Miss Lockwood, their homeroom and history teacher.

"Don't forget that midterms start two weeks after you get back," she said.

"Party pooper," Phoebe muttered.

Emily was already filled with dread about exams. She had turned into a typical Bromley grind, agonizing over her homework until late at night, trying to collect Veegees.

"No pizza for me today," Phoebe said. Instead of heading uptown to Sal's Pizza Pie Parlor, she took off in the direction of the Eighty-sixth Street Crosstown bus stop. "I still have a few pounds to lose before the class dance."

It was obvious that Phoebe had put herself on a diet. She never ate doughnuts or Cheez-Its or other fattening foods anymore. Her clothes were already loose; Emily didn't think she needed to lose more weight. Maybe she didn't have a twenty-two-inch waist or model-thin thighs, but her copper hair was as glossy as a newly minted penny and her dimples showed when she was just chewing gum. Even Emily's mother, who was the most critical person in the world, thought Phoebe was cute.

"Look, I'm smoking!" Emily said, aiming cottony puffs at Phoebe. It was phony smoke, of course—vapor produced by the mingling of warm air with the cold. They'd been studying how that happens in science class. They probably weren't going to start smoking until eleventh grade. That's when most of the girls tried it. Seniors even got to sit at a special smoking table in the cafeteria.

"You're acting like a fourth grader!" Phoebe sniffed. The comment took Emily by surprise, even though there was no doubt that Phoebe had been acting strange lately. Yesterday, in the cafeteria, she ate lunch at Cressida's table and there was no room for Emily. She spent study hall at a desk across the room from Emily's and there was no way to pass notes. She could still come to Sal's, even if she skipped the pizza. Last week, she had ordered a sugar-free ginger ale.

Phoebe was already on the bus and the doors were sliding shut when Emily climbed on. She was hungry. She'd been counting on pizza at Sal's.

"Wait up!" screeched a high-pitched voice behind her. It belonged to another classmate, Alice Unger. She was one of those annoyingly clingy girls who never seem to realize when they're not wanted. She was still a half a block away. She signaled for the driver to wait, but of course he just drove off.

Out the window, Emily saw Alice's face drop. Her mouth closed tightly over a double row of tarnished braces. Emily shouldn't have left her like that, she thought. Especially since Phoebe had rushed ahead as if to get rid of her. And was it her imagination, or did Phoebe pull away when Emily sat next to her? Was Phoebe giving Emily what her mother would call the cold shoulder?

Lady Lenore probably wouldn't mind that a bit. She wanted Emily to be friendly with Alice. One reason was that she lived in the same apartment building, even though Manhattan wasn't a suburb like Great Woods and Emily didn't have to be driven everywhere. Another reason was that Alice was Jewish. Emily wasn't sure how her mother knew that. Like Winter, Unger wasn't a typically Jewish name. But Emily's mother had a sixth sense about who was Jewish and who wasn't. She unearthed the Jewish roots behind bleached hair and changed names and fixed noses.

"Do you still need help with that phone call?" Phoebe shouted over the squeals of younger students roughhousing in the seats behind her. "Because I'm not sure I have the time."

"I can manage by myself, I guess," Emily said. But her suspicions were confirmed. Until now, Phoebe had always been so eager to help. She usually loved it when Emily asked for advice about anything connected with Bromley. "After all, I've been here since kindergarten," she liked to remind her.

Maybe it had something to do with her diet. Being hungry all the time would make anybody grumpy.

"I have to pack," Phoebe said. She was planning to visit her father over vacation. Emily hadn't met Bryce Barrett III yet. He'd been studying hawk migration patterns in the Adirondacks since school began.

Emily concentrated on squeezing her bus pass back into her wallet—it was so stuffed, she could barely snap it shut. "But what about *Rebel?*" she asked. She and Phoebe were supposed to see it on Saturday.

"Oops, I guess I forgot to tell you. My mother won't let me see a movie about juvenile delinquents. And we need a grownup to take us. You can't just sneak in. There's a matron."

The matron, stout and forbidding in a white uniform, waved a flashlight to catch children who tried to sneak in without a grown-up, or who sat in the kiddie section with cheap tickets when they were older than twelve.

"But we've been planning to see it forever!" Emily said. Besides, that was why they wanted to see the movie—because it was about crazy, mixed-up teenagers.

And now Emily was worried about something else. "You are coming to my birthday party, aren't you?"

Phoebe lowered her eyes. "I might still be away."

Emily was turning fourteen over vacation. Her parents planned to take her to a Broadway matinee with Phoebe, Alice, and Melissa. But if Phoebe didn't come, what kind of party would it be?

Before worries about Phoebe butted in, Emily had been looking forward to her birthday and two whole weeks without homework. She'd even been excited about the baby. The earth-shattering event was supposed to take place over vacation.

The bus lurched toward Park Avenue. Emily got up. "Where do you think you're going?" Phoebe asked. "I'm leaving soon—maybe even tomorrow. What about that boy you plan to invite to the class dance? If you want to work on that phone script, you should come home with me now."

Emily had met someone her second time at Flora Freund's. His name was Ted Margolin. He was a tenth grader at Kensington, Bromley's brother school. She had landed on him during the Paul Jones round. The boys stood in the outer circle and the girls on the inside. The circles moved in opposite directions while Dora, the pianist, played a bouncy march. When the music stopped, you had to dance with the person directly in front of you. Emily had landed on a tall, black-haired boy with a scar shaped like a comma across one cheek. He loved the waltz, he said, and so did she.

2 ❀ Hand-Me-Downs

Phoebe's building didn't have an elevator man like Emily's. The girls scrunched into the narrow self-service elevator next to a pimply delivery boy with a wagon from the A&P.

"Fritz, behave!" Phoebe scolded when she opened the door to apartment 4A. Her pet dachshund jumped all over Emily. His twig-like tail twitched like Mr. Carslake's metronome. "I have to take him for his walk. Why don't you wait here? I mean, because it's so cold outside."

"I don't mind," Emily said. Walking Fritz was one of Phoebe's many responsibilities. She had a bunch of them—serious chores like the heroines in books, not the fake, made-up kind Emily's mother doled out as if they were favors, like taking in the milk bottles and egg cartons from the service entrance. Phoebe had to dust the living room furniture and pick up clothes at the dry cleaner. Many nights she even started dinner. Sometimes Emily felt sorry for her. It wasn't fair for her mother to spend so many hours volunteering in a public school. Why couldn't she leave whenever she wanted to, as Lady Lenore had done when she helped out with the Great Woods winter carnival?

"Get a move on, slowpoke!" Phoebe urged, as she dragged Fritz against the wind past Riverside Drive and 116th Street. Powerful gusts whipped down the path leading to the Hudson River. It was the windiest intersection in the city—it had to do with the two curved buildings facing each other on the corner of Claremont Avenue, Phoebe said. Fritz had trouble keeping up. Dachshunds just weren't fast runners.

Phoebe's rubber-soled oxfords landed in dull thuds. No one in Great Woods would be caught dead in lace-up shoes past the age of nine. Emily's penny loafers kept slipping off as she tried to keep up.

"Here, you take him," Phoebe said. She handed the dog to Emily. Pulling up on his leash, Emily flopped down on a bench and watched Phoebe run back and forth, up and down the street. This wasn't the Phoebe Emily knew. That girl took the bus for a distance of five blocks and hated gym even more than Current Events.

Emily handed Fritz back to Phoebe. He panted heavily as they raced home against the wind. "Time to put in the bird!" Phoebe announced, running into the kitchen. Emily watched as she lifted a raw chicken from a brown wrapper, sprinkled it with paprika and dropped it in a grease-spattered pan.

"What are you gawking at? Haven't you seen a naked chicken before?" Holding a match to the pilot light, Phoebe lowered the pan into the oven.

"Of course I have," Emily lied. She'd only seen the cooked version, when Harriet, the Winters' maid, removed it from the oven, all crisp and golden.

"It'll take about an hour," Phoebe said as she and Emily stretched out on the frayed couch in the living room.

Or rather, Emily stretched out. Phoebe was doing jumping jacks.

"Stop it, already!" Emily begged. "You're making me nervous!" All that exercise was to burn up calories, she assumed.

"Just ten more." But it was more like twenty. When she was done, Phoebe positioned herself at the edge of the couch as if to spring up any second and do twenty more. Sprigs of fluff poked up from the seat cushion like weeds. How old was that couch, anyway? At least as ancient as the rumpled, balding Oriental rug that stretched across the living room floor, Emily figured.

There was no point in looking for a coaster when she set

down a glass of water on the coffee table. It was already stained with overlapping semicircles. But she was careful not to spill anything on Phoebe's parents' copy of the New York Social Register, where the name "Barrett" came right before "Barrymore."

It's not that Emily thought all the people listed in that book would be millionaires, but she still couldn't get over how shabby the Barretts' apartment was. Even their Christmas tree looked as if it had been used before. She hadn't expected to find a gigantic, gaudy tree like the one at the Dime Savings Bank where she had just deposited twelve dollars into her savings account, but the stooped specimen squatting in a corner, with a wrinkled silver star and only a few colored balls—one of them was cracked—made her sad. The Barretts obviously didn't lug home a tall, fresh evergreen—a parent at either end—like those families in pictures in magazines.

Phoebe's room was as dilapidated as the rest of the house, except for a bowl filled with marble hearts in pastel colors, which perked up the scratched dark wood dresser with drawers that didn't close.

Emily found herself longing for one of those marble hearts, especially a pink one. Maybe Phoebe would get her one for her birthday. She could use it as a paperweight. It would be the perfect way to anchor stray scraps of paper. Lady Lenore was always nagging her about the mess on her desk.

The dresser with the bowl of hearts had belonged to her grandmother, Phoebe had told her. "Grandmum Barrett moved in and shared my room when she was dying of cancer."

"Were you home when she died?" Emily asked.

"No, I had school, but she died in this room. When I came home there was a sheet over her head. It was pretty creepy."

Emily shivered slightly.

"But enough of that," Phoebe said, to Emily's relief. "High time we got to work!" She ripped a page from behind the "English" divider in her loose-leaf binder, drew a dividing line with a ruler and headed one column "Emily" and the other "Ted."

"The first time you call a boy's the hardest," she said. "After that, it's a lead-pipe cinch."

Emily found herself hoping the next call wouldn't be until the tenth-grade dance.

"The maid will probably pick up the phone, but if it's his mother, be extra polite," Phoebe continued. "Boys' mothers flip over girls with good manners."

"I'm the one who picks up the phone at my house. And what if they don't have a maid?"

"Most people do."

The Barretts were an obvious exception, but Emily didn't say anything. "Let's assume his maid—or, okay, his mother—says, 'Hello?' then, 'TED!'" Phoebe imitated Ted's mother in a shrill, high-pitched voice that sounded suspiciously like Emily's own mother's. "Or maybe she'll just go fetch him in his room."

The only boy's room Emily had ever been in was Davy Hirsch's. It was set up like a laboratory, with chemistry sets, a Bunsen burner, and a poster of his idol, Albert Einstein.

Ted's room would be more sophisticated, Emily was sure. It would have sports trophies and Ivy League pennants and pictures of Natalie Wood or Grace Kelly, or maybe Carol Lynley, the pale-haired *Seventeen* model who lived on grapes and melba toast.

"Then all you have to do is find a topic of conversation," Phoebe said. "It's easy. Break the ice with a joke. But not a knock-knock—they're too corny."

Emily winced. Her father was the king of knock-knock jokes. He laughed so hard when he told them he could hardly get the punch line out.

"Or the weather's a safe topic—and they're predicting snow!"

"Our elevator man goes on and on about the weather. It's boring."

"Well, I wouldn't bring up school or exams," Phoebe said. "You don't want him to think all you do is study. How about a movie? I know—*The Court Jester*! Because of the sword fights."

"Maybe," Emily said. She and Phoebe had agreed that the movie, which was set in the Middle Ages, had too many wisecracks about their favorite era. It would make sense to bring it up, though. At Flora Freund's, Ted had mentioned he was on the Kensington fencing team.

"So what does this Ted look like, anyway?" Phoebe asked.

"You wouldn't call him drop-dead handsome," Emily said. "His eyebrows are too thick." Just picturing him gave her a case of the butterflies.

"Do they meet across the top of his nose?"

Emily tried to remember.

"Because it's really icky if they do," Phoebe said.

Maybe they did touch, just slightly, Emily worried. "He has a cleft in his chin, though."

"Like L.O.'s?"

"Almost. And he has a scar. Just below his left cheekbone. Shaped like a comma."

Phoebe raised her eyebrows. "From an accident?"

"Maybe from fencing. He's on the Kensington team."

"Fencers don't use real swords, silly! Not like knights."

"Well, he is kind of chivalrous," Emily said. That night at Flora Freund's, he had used his handkerchief to mop up a cupful of Hawaiian Punch Emily had spilled on the dance floor. The punch bowl was the main attraction and, during breaks between dance numbers, everyone shoved their way to it.

"Maybe he had a tumor removed, like the hero in *Death Be Not Proud*," Emily continued. The book had been on the ninth-grade summer reading list.

"Em, you do have a vivid imagination! How about he was in an airplane crash and was the sole survivor?" Phoebe said. She jumped up and ran into the kitchen. "I almost forgot to feed Fritz!"

"What about us?" Emily was famished. She still hadn't eaten lunch. After school, even if they had pizza, she and Phoebe often went through a whole package of Cheez-Its or Mallomars. And usually Phoebe fed Fritz a can of disgusting-looking dog glop. But this time she emptied a bowl of spaghetti and meatballs into his dish.

"Stale leftovers," Phoebe said when she caught Emily staring. She raised the freezer's heavy lid and removed a pint of butter pecan ice cream. The Barretts' freezer wasn't part of the refrigerator. It was a separate piece of equipment made of hospital-green metal and shaped like a coffin.

"This is for you, Emily!" Phoebe said.

"Can't! I'm allergic to nuts," Emily said.

"Too bad. Looks like this is your lucky day, Fritzy." Phoebe mixed the ice cream with the spaghetti. "If there's ice cream around, I'll eat it, and there's three hundred calories in just one scoop." They were studying the digestive system in biology and Phoebe was already an expert on the calorie content of various foods.

"Not everyone can be like you—gobble everything in sight and never put on an ounce!" she said accusingly.

"Maybe you're carrying this diet thing a little too far, Pheebs. You look thin enough to me," Emily said. Phoebe's Bromley uniform had begun to sag around her hips.

"I'm not! Not yet! Philomene only weighs 112 pounds. She weighed the same twenty-five years ago when she danced on Vassar's Daisy Chain. She watches her weight and now I do, too."

"Philomene?"

"My mother—Philomene Barrett," Phoebe said.

"Since when do you call your mother by her first name?" Emily asked.

"Since just about forever."

Emily tried to picture Phoebe watching the needle on the scale as it quivered to a halt at a higher number than she wanted it to. "I have to fit into Cousin Millie's old party dresses. I just have to!" she said.

Emily had heard more than enough about Phoebe's cousin Millicent, a paragon of beauty and athletic prowess from Beacon Hill in Boston. She'd been debutante of the year in 1949. Boys had crouched outside her townhouse just to catch a glimpse of her on her way out for the evening. She'd had shoeboxes overflowing with love letters and won umpteen blue ribbons in something called equestrian dressage. An end table in the Barretts' living room displayed a framed cover of an October 1950 issue of *Life* magazine with a picture of her on horseback, flaxen hair fanning out from beneath a black velvet riding cap. She'd been killed jumping hurdles in a show a few months later. The horse hadn't cleared the highest fence.

"Millie's debutante gown was made by a famous French *couturier*," Phoebe said. She trilled the first R in *couturier*. "We have a whole closet full! If I fit into them, I won't have to wear the little girl clothes Mummy, I mean Philomene, brings home."

"Why don't you try some of them on?" Emily suggested. "If they fit, you won't have to lose more weight."

She was puzzled. Did Phoebe's mother actually bring home clothing from the public school where she volunteered? Those clothes would probably be even more worn looking than those at the Bromley-Chatham Exchange, a resale shop where students from Bromley and Chatham Academy, a rival girls' school, traded in outgrown uniforms for ones in decent condition in the next size.

That's where Phoebe's faded uniforms came from. They still had nametapes from a tenth grader named Pamela Prescott, but it occurred to Emily that Phoebe was no longer Pamela's size.

"I guess you'll be wearing a poodle skirt to the dance," Phoebe said.

Emily shook her head. Where did she get that idea? "It wouldn't be dressy enough. Besides, my skirt doesn't have a poodle on it." It had a Scottie, like the stuffed animal Emily still slept with. She'd begged her mother for that skirt when she'd seen it in the window at Gert's Glad Rags at the Great Woods shopping center last year. She'd probably outgrown that skirt. And Phoebe had never seen it. Why would she assume that's what Emily would wear to the dance?

"Excuse me, but I have to pee again," Phoebe announced. Emily heard the boing of the bathroom scale, followed by a series of thumps. More jumping jacks, she figured. She wandered into the kitchen. Fritz had licked his dish clean. Peering through the oven door, she could see that the chicken had gotten darker, but how could you tell for sure if it was ready?

An open aerogram lay next to the drainboard. It was addressed to Phoebe, and a SWAK in coral lipstick had been blotted across the flap. Left there accidentally on purpose, just begging to be looked at, Emily thought. Maybe it had to do with her favorite television program, *Dragnet*—but the show's detective, Sgt. Joe Friday, would never pass up a piece of evidence like that.

She picked up the letter and read,

Hiya Pheebs,

Guess what? My parents are splitting up. Thank the Lord, and pass the ammunition! (Get it? Remember how they used to fight—all they needed was a shotgun!!!) So here I am in sunny Reno, Nevada. We have to live here for a while because they allow you to get divorced quickly. In New York, a detective has to take pictures of your parents committing adultery, which, needless to say, is out of the question.

By the way, I'm going to public school. It's coed! Girls in junior high wear lipstick every day, the kind you have to blot, not that useless Tangee!!!!)

2 good
2 be
―――――
4 gotten

Until hell freezes over,
Your best friend 4-ever,
Juliet E. Dunne

Phoebe had never mentioned this Juliet what's-her-face, but clearly Emily was just a substitute for her. Phoebe missed Juliet. Maybe that's why she sometimes seemed so distant. As she slipped the letter back behind the phone, Emily found herself wondering if Juliet's parents had committed adultery.

"I lost six more pounds!" Phoebe announced triumphantly. She ran out of the bathroom. "Come, I'm ready to try on some of Millie's clothes!"

But just as she opened the special closet devoted to those revered hand-me-downs, her mother stormed in. With a terse nod in Emily's direction, she made a beeline for the freezer.

"Where's the ice cream?" Philomene Barrett asked shrilly. She sounded just like Phoebe's imitation of Ted's mother. "I could swear I brought home a pint from Schrafft's yesterday!"

"Uh-oh, another miserable day at work," Phoebe whispered. "Before Christmas Philomene has to work even longer hours and she gets these sugar cravings."

"Phoebe, you ate it, didn't you? I thought you wanted to fit into Millicent's dresses!" Mrs. Barrett said, as if Emily weren't standing right in front of her.

"For your information, I lost ten pounds already!" Phoebe shrieked back. "And I grew two inches over the summer. I'm taller than you now. And since you're supposed to gain five pounds for each inch, that means I actually lost *twenty* pounds!"

The freezer slammed shut. Phoebe burst into tears. Fritz took cover under the living room couch.

Emily grabbed her coat and scarf and what little they'd finished of the phone call script and raced out the door.

3 ❀ Poodle Skirts

Alice called almost as soon as Emily got home. The next bus must have come right away. "How about going to the Peachtree tomorrow?" she asked perkily.

Emily could tell she was putting up a brave front about having been left at the bus stop. But why not go? Phoebe was on her way to the Adirondacks and Emily had nothing else to do.

Before Phoebe had started her diet, she and Emily had gone to the Peachtree Coffee Shop almost as often as Sal's. Perched on the corner above the bus stop at Madison Avenue and Eighty-Eighth Street, it had two stories. Emily and Alice climbed the stairs to the top floor, which Phoebe called the loge, because she thought that watching people waiting for the bus through the plate-glass windows was a little like watching a movie.

Today Emily was fascinated by people's feet—in oxfords, saddle shoes, white bucks, loafers, businessmen's wingtips. Two pairs of kid-sized Keds were scuffing and scraping next to a grown-up's high-heeled patent leather pumps.

She and Alice had just ordered black-and-white ice cream sodas when several pairs of oxfords and sneakers approached, then disappeared through the door.

"To continue with the meeting we started in the library when we were so rudely interrupted by a certain Miss 'Spoilsport' Lockwood . . ." a familiar voice rang out.

"I could swear that's Cressida," Alice said. "I guess she hasn't left yet. I heard she was going skiing in the Alps with her mother and the latest stepfather candidate."

Emily peered over the railing. It was Cressida, all right, sliding into a booth almost directly beneath her. She sprang back.

Cressida ordered five cheeseburgers, two cherry Cokes, and three ice cream sodas, which meant there had to be at least four girls besides her.

"Nothing for me," one of the others said. Emily recognized the lilting voice. It belonged to Phoebe. So she hadn't left for the Adirondacks yet, after all. Before her diet, Phoebe had ordered chocolate ice cream sodas. Emily had always paid for Phoebe's order. She'd discreetly hand over the money for both of them as if it was the most natural thing. Phoebe didn't get a real allowance—just a dime a day in case she had to make an emergency call from a phone booth.

"The meeting about the you-know-what girls?" honked a voice that belonged to a girl named Margery Fiske. She always sounded as if she had a cold. "The girls who wear poodle——"

Alice's loud slurps drowned her out. "Shh, I want to hear this," Emily said.

"Would those girls be the Jewish girls?" asked a whispery voice that could only be Holly Gleason's. She was the dumbest girl in the class. Everyone knew she'd been accepted at Bromley only because her mother and grandmother had gone there.

"Well, well," Cressida said. "You deserve a 'Distinguished' for that! Weren't we talking about those felt skirts they wear? The ones with the gaudy poodles on them? Gail and Barbara wear them and I'm sure that new girl Emily has one, too."

Emily had almost nothing to do with Gail Roth and Barbara Kaplan, mainly because they were each other's best friends. They spoke in whispers, heads touching. They raised their hands at the same time and finished each other's answers.

"Actually, Emily's felt skirt doesn't have a poodle on it," Phoebe said. "It has a Scottie."

"You saw it?" Cressida asked.

"No, she told me."

Emily could feel the color drain from her face. She shuddered when she thought of how close she'd come to wearing her Scottie skirt on the first day of school. She'd checked the dress requirements in the Bromley Rulebook one last time: charcoal gray gym suit with matching overskirt. A black or navy belt no thicker than 1½ inches. A white shirt with a Peter Pan or button-down collar. Gray or navy kneesocks.

But that first morning she'd noticed a sentence she hadn't read before. "For special occasions, a non-uniform skirt in gray, navy blue, or plaid—but never a straight skirt—may be worn instead of the overskirt." Wasn't the first day of school a special occasion? Wouldn't the other girls be wearing non-uniform skirts over their gym suits? And she had the perfect skirt hanging in her closet. Her Scottie skirt was blue. She removed it from its hanger and pulled it over her gym suit.

But what if she was the only one wearing a different skirt? That would be embarrassing beyond belief. She changed back into the uniform skirt.

"What's taking so long?" Lady Lenore said, shuffling in with her belly leading the way. It was blown up like a blimp, a constant reminder that Emily's only-child status was about to end.

There was no time to change again.

"How do you know for sure that Emily's Jewish?" Phoebe was asking.

"My mother says so," said Cressida.

Emily tried to remember if she and Phoebe had ever discussed their religions. The Jewish holidays, Rosh Hashanah and Yom Kippur, had come early this year. They were over before Bromley began, so Emily didn't have to miss any school. And Lord Sidney said their last name sounded like the name of a British aristocrat. It had been changed from an unpronounceable Polish name starting with a W when Emily's grandfather first came to America.

"Winter!" the immigration officer had said, stamping Grandpa Herman's passport.

"I wish *I* had a poodle skirt," Holly said.

"My mother says they're vulgar," said Cressida.

"I've never actually seen Gail and Barbara in skirts like that," Phoebe said. "Since when don't they have to wear our disgusting uniform to school like the rest of us?"

"But have you noticed how they always have to have brand-new uniforms?" Cressida said. "Like they're too good to wear their older sisters' or buy used ones. That new girl you're so friendly with—her skirt is so dark, it's almost black."

"Come on, Cress, you get plenty of new clothes every year!" said a mellow-voiced girl named Lindsley McGovern.

"But they're not flashy."

"I wouldn't mind having a new uniform for a change," Phoebe said. "Mine have been washed so many times, they're all faded."

Emily had noticed that Phoebe's uniforms were several shades lighter than hers.

"They can't mean me. I always wear Bettina's old uniforms," Alice whispered. Bettina, her older sister, had graduated from Bromley the year before.

Emily leaned over the railing again. This time she spotted Lindsley's ski-jump nose and Eugenia Stamos's black headband nestled in her dark brown hair. She had been one of the most stricken of the James Dean mourners.

"What about Alice?" Lindsley said. "She wears kilts even though she's Jewish. Do we have to stop talking to her?"

Alice looked as if she'd been slapped in the face. "We're not really Jewish," she said. "We don't do anything Jewish. I've never even been to temple or whatever you call a Jewish church."

"So how come they know you're Jewish?" Emily asked.

"Maybe she said 'newish.'"

"Yeah, sure." But Emily couldn't believe what she was hearing either. This was no ordinary clique. Not like the one at Great Woods last year, where some sixth graders got suspended for picking on girls with freckles. When they noticed that Emily had a brown fleck in one of her blue eyes, they made fun of her, too.

"It just so happens that I kind of like those poodles with the rhinestone eyes and the fancy haircuts," Emily heard Phoebe say.

She was sticking up for her, Emily thought with relief.

"Lindsley has a real poodle with a fancy haircut!" Holly said.

"Everybody adores our darling Gigi!" said Lindsley, making kissing noises.

"We are not discussing dogs!" Cressida said impatiently. "Kindly stick to the subject. We're talking about *girls*—girls who are different. Mother says they have their own customs, their own way of dressing. They're show-offy. Everything has to be loud and shiny. Like those rhinestones on their poodle skirts. And they buy lots of them. That's why I call them the 'Clothes Girls.'"

"The Clothes Girls! What a perfect name!" Margery said with a hoarse giggle.

"They even have television sets in their bedrooms. And their own pastel-colored telephones," Cressida went on.

"I wish we had a television," Phoebe said. "Or at least a radio. All we have is a phonograph. My parents expect me to listen to classical records or read great works of literature all day long."

Phoebe had once watched *I Love Lucy* with Emily on her parents' television console. Lucy had been performing a dance routine with a dummy of Ricky. Phoebe had rolled on the floor in hysterics.

"I was invited to play at Barbara's house in fourth grade, but my mother wouldn't let me go," Lindsley said. "Could it be because she's Jewish?"

"I wouldn't be a bit surprised," Cressida said. "Mother told me families from that background aren't allowed to live in our apartment building. And none of those girls go to Miss Thornberry's. They have to wear those poodle skirts to their own dancing school. And when they're in college, they can't be debutantes. They can't be listed in the Social Register. You're not allowed to invite them to coming-out parties at the Colonial Club, so what's the point of being friendly with them?"

"Who cares about deb parties?" Lindsley said. "It's dumb to be introduced to your parents' friends when you've known them all your life."

"I can't wait to be a debutante!" Eugenia boomed. "You get to wear a long white gown like a bride, and you have a million escorts! I'll make my debut at the International Ball, like the other Greek shipowners' daughters."

Emily saw the people at the next table turn around.

"That's only because Greek girls aren't invited to the more important dances and you know it," Cressida said. She banged a knife on the table. "From now on, we are to have nothing to do with the Clothes Girls!'

"I don't believe this!" Alice said, gagging on her soda. "Besides, Lindsley came to my ninth birthday party."

"It is pretty unbelievable," Emily agreed. She felt sick.

"I herewith declare the formation of the Anti–Clothes Girl League!" Cressida announced. "Who will second my motion?"

"But what about Bromley's rule about no clubs outside of school?" Phoebe said.

"That moronic old rule!" Cressida said scornfully. "Anyway, the ACGL won't be a club. It'll be more like a league—like the medieval merchant associations we've been studying in history."

"Like the Hanseatic League?" Margery asked.

"Exactly. Who could possibly object to that?"

"But Barbara and Gail have been in our class since kindergarten, and Alice came in first grade," Phoebe said. "Besides, you're forgetting about another rule: we're supposed to help new girls like Emily."

"Tough! Whose side are you on anyway?" Cressida said. "None of those girls should've been accepted, so it's up to us to un-accept them. If the best apartment buildings and the best dancing school in the city don't let in Jews, why should the best school? Chatham, which isn't half as good, doesn't accept Jewish girls."

Just then Alice hiccupped loudly. Lindsley and Margery glanced up. Emily and Alice ducked under the table.

"Attention, please! I repeat, who will second my motion?" Cressida asked.

"Me! I second it!" Margery boomed.

"I third it!" said Holly.

"You are so out of it!" Cressida said. "You don't *third* a motion. Next is all in favor, say aye!"

"Aye," echoed Eugenia and Lindsley.

"Aye—I guess," said Phoebe. So much for her feeble attempts to protest, Emily thought.

"I just wish we had better initials," Margery was saying. "Letters that form a word, like the WACs. My aunt served with them in World War II."

"My mother belongs to the Daughters of the American Revolution," Holly said. "It's called the DAR. That's not a word."

"Good point. Our club, I mean league, will be known as the ACGL, and that's final," Cressida said.

A hum of agreement followed. "Our business is concluded," Cressida said. "Fellow leaders of the ACGL, I'll be thinking of you on the slopes!"

Emily watched Cressida and the others straggle out in their camel hair coats and striped scarves.

"Looks like your best friend now belongs to a club that won't let her speak to you," Alice said with a hint of pleasure.

"Rub it in, why don't you?" Why did friends—and Emily had to admit that Alice was becoming a friend—sometimes gloat over one another's troubles? "She had no choice. I would be afraid of Cressida, too."

In Phoebe's place, Emily was pretty sure she would have sat there without a peep of protest.

"Go ahead and make excuses for her. I couldn't care less," Alice said. "But I'd be plenty hurt, if I were you."

Emily was hurt, there was no doubt about it. But she found it hard to believe that the Phoebe who had joined Cressida's league was the real Phoebe. The real Phoebe spent an afternoon with Emily writing to the Laurence Olivier Fan Club in London to send away for a poster of L.O. The real Phoebe took Emily to see the suits of armor at the Metropolitan Museum. The real Phoebe liked to pretend that Central Park was Avalon and that she and Emily were members of King Arthur's court.

"I have an idea," Alice said, winding a green and white scarf around her stubby neck. It was from Dartmouth, her father's college. "I should invite those girls over to see our certificate from the *St. Charles,* the ship my ancestors sailed on. It proves that some Jewish people came to America a year after the Pilgrims on the same kind of boat as the *Mayflower,* only nicer."

Alice just didn't get it, Emily thought. She refused to see the obvious, maybe because it was too hurtful. Those girls would probably never come to her house again.

4 ❀ Ornaments

"Where's your tree?" Phoebe asked.

She had come to Emily's birthday party after all. She and Alice were the only guests. Melissa was home in Great Woods with the German measles. They were sitting on the black leather couch in the Winters' living room, under the black-and-white painting that looked like a Rorschach inkblot.

"We haven't put it up yet," Emily said.

The words just spilled out and there was no way to pull them back. Tomorrow her father would light the first Chanukah candle. The Winters never had a Christmas tree. Her mother was out of earshot in the kitchen, checking with Harriet about the egg salad sandwiches and the chocolate frosted birthday cake they would have for lunch.

"Our tree's been up for ages!" Alice bragged. "We have tons of new ornaments. The cutest Rudolph you'd ever want to see!"

Many Jews had Christmas trees, so Phoebe might have expected Emily to have one, too. One of the many annoying things about Alice was the way she was always bragging. "My father's a partner at Caldwell, Unger, Grant, and McInerney," she'd once boasted, without bothering to ask what Emily's father did.

"Are those real diamonds?" Phoebe asked, pointing to a border of glittery stones at the hem of Emily's brown velvet skirt. Emily had forgotten about those stones. They weren't as big or bright as the glittery eyes on her Scottie skirt, but they still sparkled. Phoebe wore a black watch plaid kilt, fastened with a silver safety pin. It hung too loosely around her waist. Emily wondered if it was one of Cousin Millie's.

"Are you serious? They're something fake, like crystal," Emily said. She wondered what Ted and the other Kensington boys wore to birthday parties. Blazers and ties? Did they go to theater matinees, too?

Emily's father tapped on the living room door. "Knock, knock!"

"Dad, pretty please, don't!" Just this time there had to be a way to stop him. Couldn't he not embarrass Emily for once in his life?

Alice was smiling. "Who's there?" She asked.

"Toby!"

For a smart man, he had the worst taste in jokes, Emily thought. And now that he had an audience, there was no stopping him.

"Oh, I know this one!" Alice said. "To-by or not to be." Her kilt shimmied up her legs, exposing a pair of husky thighs.

"You Bromley girls think you're so smart, but I'll trick you yet!" Lord Sidney said, exhaling a foul-smelling spiral of smoke. In his smoking jacket, puffing on a cigar, he looked like Edward G. Robinson, who happened to be Jewish.

Emily's parents always knew which movie stars were Jewish. Lauren Bacall was Jewish. So was Paul Muni, an actor from before Emily was born. Cary Grant was half Jewish. Debbie Reynolds converted to marry Eddie Fisher, a Jewish singer.

Lord Sidney pointed his cigar at a painting over the mantelpiece. "See this exquisite work of art?"

The painting showed a woman's back naked from the waist up, but you could see the slope of one breast as she faced a mirror, brushing her hair. "A lady at her *toilette*," he said. He was about to demonstrate how the painting turned into a landscape when you hung it upside down. He did this whenever people came over. He had done it in Great Woods, too.

This time there had to be a way to stop him.

"Dad, pretty please, don't!" Emily begged. But he had already unhooked the painting and was hanging it back horizontally.

"Okay! What do you see now?" he asked.

"A clown putting on whiteface!" Alice said with confidence.

"The Alps in the summertime tipped with snow?" Phoebe asked tentatively.

"Gotcha! It's a village on the Riviera! See the azure Mediterranean over there?"

"Sidney, you're flicking ashes all over the marble!" Lady Lenore said. Sooty specks dotted the white squares on the checkerboard floor.

It was no use, Emily thought. Everything about her parents was embarrassing. Her father's knock-knocks. The reversible painting. That giant television console in the bedroom. And her mother—*especially* her mother—with her belly blown up like a float in the Thanksgiving Day parade.

There was something embarrassing about being Jewish, too, it seemed. Jewish features, like bumpy noses and frizzy hair, weren't considered attractive. They had to be fixed or straightened or covered up. There was even something known as Jewish thighs. They rubbed up against each other and made you need a girdle.

"Luncheon is served!" Emily's mother announced. She flung open the dining room door as if to usher guests into the ballroom at Buckingham Palace, her belly leading the way.

At the center of the table an arrangement of pink sweetheart roses was flanked by tiny salt shakers with dollhouse-sized spoons. Parfait glasses stuffed with carrots and celery sticks stood at either end. The good plates, the ones with the blue roses and matching napkins embroidered with identical blue roses, had been placed at each setting. Lady Lenore jangled the silver bell she had taken to summoning Harriet with, even though the kitchen connected with the dining room. The salt shakers and the bell embarrassed Emily. The fancy china and the napkins, too. She could imagine what Phoebe must be thinking.

Harriet passed around a platter of sandwiches with the

crusts trimmed away. Emily watched Phoebe. She didn't touch the egg salad. She nibbled on the carrots and celery. When the cake was served, she mushed it around her plate, spreading it so thin it almost disappeared into the blue roses.

"Knock, knock," Emily's father said again. He was standing at the door with his mouth filled with egg salad. "Who's there? / Alfred / Alfred who? / A-fred of gaining weight? I made that one up!"

"Please, Sidney, can't you see you're embarrassing Emily?" her mother said. That only embarrassed Emily more.

Later, Emily watched from the third row as Anne Frank and her family hid out from the Nazis in an attic in Amsterdam. Anne was only thirteen. When she blotted her lipstick and draped her mother's crocheted shawl around her shoulders for her visit with Peter van Damm, the teenaged boy whose family had moved into the attic with the Franks, Emily pictured herself sneaking away to meet Ted. They would have more privacy, of course; Ted's room would be a real room, not a tiny space carved out of an attic. Emily got goose bumps just thinking about being alone there with him.

Onstage, Peter was saying that he would never tell anyone he was Jewish after the war was over. She wouldn't do anything like that, Emily told herself. Pretending she would have a Christmas tree was a lie, but she wasn't pretending *not* to be Jewish. She just wasn't shouting it from the highest rooftop.

During intermission, her mother passed out Almond Joys. Emily saw Phoebe slip hers into her pocket. "I'm not hungry right now," she said.

In the third act, the Nazis discovered the Franks' hiding place. As they rushed up the stairs to the attic, Anne and Peter kissed passionately for the first and last time. The actress who played Anne blinked back tears as she took her curtain call.

"She's still sad from the play," Phoebe said.

"She overacted," said Alice. "The way she tossed that stupid shawl over her shoulders and strutted around Peter. I mean, would you do that?"

She might have, Emily thought. Of course, no one wore shawls like that anymore. But the actor who played Peter was handsome. With his shock of dark hair, he reminded her of Laurence Olivier. And of Ted Margolin, too.

"I wonder if Anne and Peter ever got married," Phoebe said with a shudder.

"I doubt it. I read somewhere that Anne was killed in one of those Nazi concentration camps," Alice said, between mouthfuls of Almond Joy.

"Why did they have to kill *Anne*? I mean, she was so young! They could have just kept her as a prisoner of war," Phoebe said.

Or maybe just snubbed her like the girls in your club would do? Emily thought of saying. Instead, she said, "Why should she be a prisoner? What did she ever do to them?"

Phoebe shrugged. "Search me."

"Maybe if Bromley didn't insist on plodding through history chronologically and we were studying World War II instead of those irrelevant Middle Ages, we'd find out," Alice said.

"My mother told me there were Americans who didn't think we should get into the war," said Phoebe.

"They didn't think we should fight Adolf Hitler?" Emily said.

"He was trying to take over Europe, not the U.S."

"Don't you think we should help other people in trouble?"

"Yes, and that's what our country did," Phoebe said. "My father tried to join the army but they wouldn't take him because he had an irregular heartbeat. Lindsley's father was killed in the war. He was a pilot. His plane was shot down. She was just a baby. She never got to know him."

"That's terrible!" Emily watched her father try to hail a cab. He hadn't served in the army because he was too near-sighted.

"So it wasn't only Jewish people who had bad things happen to them," Phoebe said.

"I know that," Alice sniffed.

Outside, the pale December sun had already slipped behind

the horizon. Anne Frank hadn't felt a breeze or witnessed a single sunset while confined in that attic. And she never had enough to eat, Emily thought, as she watched Phoebe toss her Almond Joy in a trashcan. What Peter van Damm would have given for a single bite of that chocolate! He was always starving. That selfish mother of his had stooped so low as to steal potato scraps meant for him. But Phoebe was starving herself on purpose.

"Where do you live, exactly?" Lord Sidney asked, flagging down a cab while Lady Lenore tried to button her sealskin coat over her belly.

"Oh, no, please, you don't have to take me all the way home," Phoebe said. "I can catch the bus near your house."

"I won't hear of it," Lord Sidney said. "Going all the way to the West Side in the dark by yourself!"

Another embarrassing comment. How did he think Phoebe got home from school every day? But there was no way out of it. Lord Sidney insisted on dropping her off. Actually, it didn't take long to get to Phoebe's neighborhood from Broadway, which happened to be on the West Side, too.

"Have fun trimming the tree," Phoebe said, as the cab pulled up in front of 25 Claremont Avenue. Emily's mother didn't turn around from where she was sitting on one of the jump seats. If she was startled by Phoebe's comment, it didn't show.

"Mmm," Emily mumbled. Why in the world was she pretending that she celebrated Christmas? It was one thing for Anne Frank's family to hide from people who wanted to kill them, another for Emily to hide who she was from a classmate who probably knew anyway.

"So this is where you live," Emily's father said. As if Phoebe lived in a trailer park. As if her family wasn't listed in the New York Social Register.

5 ❀ Crutches

1163 Park Avenue, the Winters' apartment building, was divided into six sections, each with its own lobby and elevator. The towers and crenellated turrets made it look like a medieval fortress, with a rock garden where a moat would be.

Alice lived on the south side of the building, in the same section as the judge who had sentenced Julius and Ethel Rosenberg, who were spies for Russia, to death. Even Emily's parents, who despised communists, had been among the many people who had written to President Eisenhower, begging him to spare the Rosenbergs' lives because they had young children, but the Rosenbergs were sent to the electric chair anyway. The judge had received death threats himself, and before Emily's family moved into the building, policemen had guarded the entrance. Everyone felt safe with those police officers outside, so now the doormen wore double-breasted, navy blue uniforms with peaked caps—just like New York City policemen.

"You'll catch your death of cold," Vince, the elevator man, warned. Emily was wearing her Bromley blazer, but all she had to do was walk across the courtyard. Besides, couldn't he mind his own business?

Vince hadn't picked up any passengers yet. Emily still felt awkward when she found another person in the elevator. Her apartment was on the eighth floor, smack in the middle of the building. Usually someone boarded before or after she did. And if it was someone she didn't like, she couldn't just get up and leave.

It wasn't as if you were expected to be friendly. Passengers said hello to the elevator man, but most of the time, they didn't greet each other. Lord Sidney went overboard, of course, tipping his hat, telling knock-knocks to anyone who would listen. Emily tried to avoid taking the elevator with him.

Just as she feared, the elevator lurched to a stop on the sixth floor. Pretty please, let it not be Cameron the Conceited! Or let it be him! Emily was never sure which to wish for. Cameron was the broodingly handsome Kensington senior who lived in 6L. He usually grunted in her direction, before hashing over the Yankees' prospects for the coming season with Vince. The possibility of seeing him both scared and excited Emily. He thought he was God's gift to women. You could tell from the way he raked his hand through his dark blond hair.

Emily felt a tinge of disappointment when Wally and Willy, the twins from 8K, boarded the elevator with their governess, Mademoiselle.

"You stink!" Wally or Willy said, pummeling his brother with his schoolbag.

"Parlez français!" Mademoiselle ordered.

"You smell like ca-ca!" Willy or Wally said, pummeling him back.

A sister wouldn't be like that, Emily hoped. Nor would Emily treat a sister that way. Vacation had been getting boring, and she found herself wishing her mother would go ahead and have the baby. Phoebe was in the Adirondacks and other classmates were in Bermuda or Vermont. This time last year, the Winters had been away too, and Emily had been practicing the butterfly stroke in the pool at the Versailles Hotel in Miami Beach, hoping the lifeguard with the rippling muscles would notice her.

She knew she should follow Miss Lockwood's advice and start studying for midterms, but she had left most of her books at school. She would have to borrow one from Alice.

"Okay, let me guess. You need a book," Alice bellowed into the phone.

Was it so obvious Emily was calling because she needed

something? "I was wondering if you brought home *Life in the Middle Ages*."

"Of course," Alice said. "And all my other books. Come on over."

Alice's apartment was really on the thirteenth floor but, for superstitious reasons, it was labeled the fourteenth. Emily almost tripped over a wheelchair parked in the vestibule. So Alice's mother was the cranky-looking crippled lady who waited at the building entrance for taxis, sometimes in the wheelchair, other times hunched over a pair of crutches.

The Ungers' apartment had the same layout as the Winters,' except that what should have been on the left was on the right, and vice versa. Emily followed the aroma of fresh pastries to the kitchen, which was to the right instead of the left of the dining room. From the doorway, she watched a woman in a blue-and-white-striped seersucker uniform remove a tray of brownies from the oven and set them to cool on the kitchen counter.

The woman glared at Emily. "Not ready yet!" she snapped.

Emily jumped back. "I forgot to warn you. Louisa has conniptions if you even come close to the kitchen," Alice said.

"We can't have any brownies?"

Alice winked. "Don't worry, I have a secret stash."

They walked past her sister Bettina's room, which corresponded to the future nursery in Emily's apartment. A do-not-disturb sign from the Waldorf-Astoria Hotel dangled from the doorknob.

Alice turned it over to the "Please make up the room" side. "She's not here for a change. She's spending the weekend with her boyfriend in Cambridge. For the Harvard-Princeton football game. He graduated from Kensington last year. His name is Kit Chadwick and he's the living end."

The whole weekend? Where was she staying? Emily wondered.

"He puts her up at the best hotel in Cambridge," Alice said, as though reading her mind.

Maybe Ted Margolin would go to Harvard. Maybe he would

invite Emily up for a football weekend. Maybe he would put her up at the best hotel. *Whoa, you're going too fast,* she told herself. You haven't even invited him to the class dance yet. Does he even know you're alive?

Alice opened the door to Bettina's room. It was larger than Alice's and not as austere. The walls were papered with a pattern of frolicking shepherds. Matching curtains hung at the window. The bedspread matched, too.

Bettina was already a Bromley legend. She got mostly Vee-gees and was captain of the field hockey team. As president of the twelfth grade, she was fighting for more joint activities with Kensington. She had applied to Wellesley as her first choice and to two other Seven Sisters colleges. "She doesn't even need a safety choice," Alice bragged.

"Everybody says she looks like Elizabeth Taylor," she continued. "Those violet eyes, they say. Now, I ask you, who has violet eyes? No one! There's no such thing! I looked it up in a medical book. Bettina's eyes are plain old boring blue. If they were violet, she'd be some kind of freak!"

"Yeah, I think they use a purple tint on Liz's eyes in the magazines," Emily said.

They tiptoed past Alice's mother's room. She was asleep. Was she sleeping late or taking an early nap? Emily wondered. Why did adults nap like babies? Her parents often slept away entire Saturday afternoons while Emily read or studied. Personally, she found it more interesting to be awake.

In Alice's room narrow, cot-like beds met in an L shape in a corner, with a small nightstand between them. Aside from a school desk with a chair attached to it classroom style, there was no other furniture. It looked like a hotel room where Alice was the guest, and not such a welcome one, Emily thought.

A ballet barre stretched along an entire wall, beneath a photograph of a young girl wreathed in scarves and doing a pirouette. "I didn't know you danced," Emily said.

"That's my mother when she was young. Not me."

So Alice's frail, disabled mother had once had sturdy, muscular legs like her daughter. What happened? Emily wondered.

Reaching into her desk drawer, Alice offered Emily a stale, crumbling brownie. "This is from the last batch."

"No, thanks," Emily said, making a face.

"Here's an even better stash!" Alice said. From under a stack of sweaters on a closet shelf, she pulled out the December 1955 issue of *Modern Romances* magazine.

On the cover, a couple was locked in a passionate embrace. Inside, the Breck Girl, looking like Cressida, showed off her freshly shampooed, wheat-colored hair.

"Don't tell me you don't like these magazines!" Alice said.

"I'm just surprised you have them," Emily said. Her mother didn't allow love magazines in the house. Alice's mother probably didn't approve of them, either, but she wasn't likely to go snooping in her wheelchair.

"Come on, don't be a prude!" Alice said. She belly-flopped on the bed. "This one sounds great: 'Beach Party Passion, or A Make-Out Session in Her Boyfriend's Convertible Spells Trouble for Suzy.'"

She read aloud,

After forcing down a spoonful of cereal, Suzy clapped a dish towel to her mouth and fled from the kitchen. In the bathroom, she turned the faucets on full force to drown out any retching sounds. She was pregnant—there was no doubt about it—"in trouble," as the town gossips would say.

What should she do? Where could she turn? She certainly couldn't fly to Switzerland or Puerto Rico, like rich girls did to take care of unwanted pregnancies. Her best friend Shirley almost bled to death when she went to the nearest city, to a student doctor without proper surgical tools. And Shirley had a reputation. She wasn't like Suzy, who worked with her father in his hardware store on Saturdays after her job as telephone operator and helped her mother with the cooking and cleaning.

Of course, it was all Ma's fault, Suzy thought bitterly, as tears coursed down her cheeks. She'd had to learn the facts of life all by herself. How many times had she asked her mother, "Ma, how far does a girl have to go to, um, get in trouble?" "Now you better behave yourself!" Her mother would answer angrily, slamming down her knitting needles or her rolling pin. "Don't let the boys get fresh!" But, in the back seat of his Thunderbird convertible, Suzy had let Kenny go too far, way too far. . . .

"I can't get over that this Suzy person didn't know how you get pregnant. Nurse Lambroza taught us in sixth-grade Health and Hygiene," Alice said. "Before you came to Bromley."

Emily found it hard to picture the school nurse, in her prissy white uniform with her cropped hair tucked inside a white cap, teaching about sex. And did Alice think Bromley was the only place to learn the facts of life?

"We learned in fifth grade," Emily said. She had found out about them from a book of Melissa's, *A Baby Is Born.*

"So how do you do on purity tests?" Alice asked.

Emily had never taken a purity test, but there was no reason for Alice to know that. The trick was not to offer too much made-up information. "Around ninety," she said.

"Aha! Just as I thought! You never took one! You earn points and a category, not a grade—like 'Pure as the driven snow' if you answer 'no' to all the questions."

Emily hid her burning cheeks behind the Breck Girl.

"Don't you go to camp?" Alice asked. "The junior counselors passed them around our bunk last summer."

"We didn't have junior counselors," Another lie. Emily had never been to sleepaway camp. It was a sore point with her mother, but she was afraid to go. Why did she find herself telling so many lies since coming to Bromley? Why did she feel she had to conceal so much of her true self?

"Our counselor Toni's score was 'No damn good if not married!' That's because she checked off 'yes' for 'Have you ever petted below the waist?' She even checked off the one about having a hickey," Alice said.

"Oh, yeah?"

"I bet you don't even know what a hickey is."

"I do so." Emily had no idea. Was it a more advanced kind of kiss?

"Even I don't know the exact definition. Let's look it up." A thick Webster's dictionary lay open on a pedestal in the living room. Alice turned the tissue-thin pages to the Hs.

"This isn't the 'hickey' I'm thinking of," she said, shaking her head. Emily peered over her shoulder. She read, "Hickey, noun. A fitting used to mount a lighting fixture in an outlet box or on a pipe."

"So you're the one who doesn't know what it means!"

"There must be two different types of hickeys. This dictionary is probably 'abridged,' and they left out the 'hickey' I'm talking about because it's too disgusting," Alice said.

"Oh, yeah, so what is your kind of hickey?"

"It's a love bite. When you do heavy petting and your boyfriend gets very 'hot,' he leaves a mark on your neck. Once our counselor Toni wore a turtleneck when it was boiling, so we knew she had a hickey."

Like vampires, Emily thought. What was fun about biting? If Ted took her out on a date, would they have to bite each other after they kissed with their tongues?

"Last year, we played kissing games at birthday parties," Emily said. She left out the part about how they had only kissed on the cheek.

"Thrills chills! We played Spin the Bottle with boys from Kensington when I was in fifth grade!" Alice said.

"We played in the dark. With candles." There was no reason for Alice to know they had used a flashlight. "And we had a kissing booth." Another lie. The only kissing booths Emily had come across were in *Archie* comic books.

"So what's so special about that?" Alice said, as they walked back to her bedroom. "I thought girls from the suburbs were, well, you know—fast. I thought they let boys feel them up and necked in sports cars and went all the way."

"And got pregnant, like Suzy?"

"Hmm. I guess it's better to be in the 'Pure as the driven snow' category, like you would be."

"What was your category, may I ask?"

"The one right above yours. I forget what it's called. Come on, let's read!"

Emily picked up the magazine. She pointed to the photograph illustrating the story. The model had a mass of black curls. "She looks Jewish, don't you think?"

Alice snatched the magazine. "Just because she has dark hair? Eugenia and Holly and other Christian girls in the class have dark hair, too. I'm not sure what you mean by 'looking Jewish.'"

She read on:

Suzy took the long bus ride to the Cradle Haven for Mothers-to-Be, a hundred miles over the state line. "We find loving families for our babies," said the directress, showing her to her room. But how could she, Suzy White, pay for one sin with another—the sin of putting her own flesh and blood up for adoption? Cross my heart and hope to die, I will find a way to raise my child, she promised herself.

"Wouldn't you hate to be cooped up in one of those unwed mothers' homes?" Alice asked. "I wonder if you're allowed to go out."

Emily had heard that in the Middle Ages even married women went into "confinement" long before they got to be as pregnant as her mother, but in this day and age, there was no reason to conceal her condition.

"I guess Suzy ends up keeping the baby," Emily said. "But if it were me, I'd probably put it up for adoption." A fleeting image of handing Eva Jane over to another family at birth made her smile.

"Sometimes I pretend I was adopted," Alice said. "It's better than what really happened."

"What are you talking about?" Emily asked.

"My mother got polio when she was pregnant with me. Her legs have been paralyzed ever since."

"But I thought polio mainly happened to children!"

Of course, Emily knew of at least one grown-up, President Franklin Delano Roosevelt, who had gotten polio. He woke up with a fever and a stiff neck one morning, and the next thing he knew his limbs were like taffy. Had Alice's mother's legs buckled under, like his?

Not so long ago, before there was a vaccine, notices about polio were posted everywhere, warning you to wash your hands but not to use other people's towels or the water fountain, and to dry off completely after a swim. There were posters of children in braces and pictures of kids in iron lungs. You could only see their heads and the drawings and get well cards taped to the top and swinging above them. Every time Emily had growing pains in her legs, she worried that it was polio. Until now, though, she'd never met anyone who'd actually caught the disease. And last year she was vaccinated, along with all the other kids in Great Woods.

After the mass vaccination, her eighth-grade teacher, Mr. Greenblatt, ripped the March of Dimes poster and all the other scary pictures off the wall, proclaiming, "One of the worst scourges known to humanity has been eliminated!"

If only the vaccine had been invented before Alice's mother got polio. "It's like it was my fault," Alice said. "I think Mother blames me."

"It's awful that your mother had polio but it is not your fault," Emily said. "She got it because it's contagious. Before the vaccine, everyone was afraid of catching it."

At the beach, her mother had made her change into a dry bathing suit the minute she got out of the water. While she held a towel around her, Emily had wanted to sink into the sand.

"But Mother wanted to be a professional dancer," Alice

said. "She studied with Martha Graham. She danced the whole time she was pregnant with Bettina."

"Well, it's very sad that she's paralyzed, but she has no right to blame you!" Having polio was no excuse for meanness, Emily thought.

"If it weren't for me, Mother would probably be as famous as Martha Graham."

Emily still found it hard to imagine Alice's sullen, wheelchair-bound mother leaping across a stage and curtsying with a bouquet of roses.

"She made me take dance lessons. Out of spite. Because she knows I have two left feet. Bettina's graceful, of course. She studies the Isadora Duncan technique. Personally, I think she's nothing but a sickening goody two-shoes."

"Me, too," Emily agreed.

She didn't blame Alice for being jealous. Bettina was much prettier, too. "Maybe they'll find a cure for people like your mother, who already had polio," she said.

"Do you think it might happen? If Mother could dance again, she might not hate me so much!"

Did Alice's mother hate her? Could a mother hate her daughter? How about a daughter hating her mother? What Emily sometimes felt for Lady Lenore was, at the very least, strong dislike, she thought later, as she crossed the courtyard with *Life in the Middle Ages* tucked under her arm. Vince had been right about the weather. She was freezing in her Bromley blazer.

6 ❀ Layette

"Pretty please, can I have a kilt?" Emily begged.

"May I," her mother corrected. They were shopping at Best & Co., Emily's least favorite store. She called it Worst & Co. The racks were hung with babyish party dresses with collars like giant doilies and spring coats with velvet trim and itchy tweed leggings. Emily and her mother used to make special trips in from Great Woods to shop here, and now—how lucky could you get?—they lived only a taxicab ride away.

But at least there were kilts. In every plaid you could think of, all with those giant safety pins.

"We'll see. Your dress for the dance is more important," Emily's mother said. If they were looking for a dance dress, what were they doing in the Lilliputian Bazaar, full of silver rattles and outfits for the Little Princess?

"But first we'll get the pram," her mother said.

Of course. How could Emily forget about the pram? Did her mother actually think she would be interested in shopping for a baby carriage? Did she even care about her opinion, for that matter? Emily had heard her on the phone with Aunt Irene, who was a friend, not a relative: "Do you think it would improve Emily's attitude if I let her help with some of the preparations?"

This trip to Best's was just a fake way to get her involved, Emily decided, like when she was in first grade and her mother asked her to help set the table, then rearranged all the cutlery when she wasn't looking.

Sure enough, Lady Lenore walked straight up to a gigantic gray carriage with the words Silver Cross in chrome script along the side. The interior was upholstered in ivory leather and lined with a matching navy blue blanket. A monogram would be embroidered on the blanket after the baby was named—Eva Jane, Emily hoped.

"What do you think?" her mother asked. She was only pretending she needed Emily's opinion. It was obvious she had already made up her mind.

"Won't such a huge carriage be hard to push up and down the curbs?" Emily asked.

"The baby nurse will do most of the pushing."

"Baby nurse?" It was the first time Emily had heard of any baby nurse.

"A woman named Hilda Wertheimer will take care of your brother or sister for the first few months. But she likes to be called Fräulein."

"Did I have a baby nurse?"

"For a while."

Liar, liar, pants on fire. Emily had never had a nurse take care of her. Grandma Anna had come over every day. There were the pictures to prove it.

"She'll be living with us until the baby sleeps through the night," her mother said. "In the baby's room, not yours."

But sharing my bathroom, Emily thought with distaste. "She sounds German. Didn't you say you don't like German people because of the Nazis?"

"She may be German, but she's no Nazi. She's Jewish. After the war many Jewish refugees came to America from Germany."

"Did we have any relatives in Germany?"

"No. We were lucky. Grandpa Herman and Grandma Anna came from Europe a long time ago."

"Have you met this Fräulein person?"

"Of course. I interviewed her."

While Emily was at school, apparently. Her mother hadn't even pretended to want to find out what she thought of her.

"Was she in one of those concentration camps?" Emily asked.

"I didn't ask her," Lady Lenore said.

"You weren't curious?"

"You don't talk about things like that."

Why? Because it was upsetting? Emily would ask Fräulein, she decided. At the right moment, of course.

Lady Lenore was checking the carriage mattress. "Very high quality," she said.

"What was my baby carriage like?" Emily asked.

"Very similar," her mother said. "I gave it to Aunt Wilma for cousin Steven. He was born a year after you."

Another lie. Emily had seen pictures of herself strapped into a plaid foldable model, the kind they sold at Sears, Roebuck & Co. Of course, that was years before her father invented Whirlex. Now her parents could afford a Packard convertible with whitewall tires, so why not a fancy pram?

In the next aisle, a woman with grayish-blond hair twisted into a bun was busy helping a young pregnant woman—who was the right age to have a baby, Emily couldn't help thinking. After folding a pink blanket, the saleslady spun around.

"That looks like Phoebe's mom!" Emily said.

"Really?" her mother said.

"I can't swear to it without my glasses."

"Then put them on, for pity's sake."

"You're the one who's always telling me not to use my glasses as a crutch!"

"That doesn't mean you shouldn't wear them when you need them."

Emily let the comment slide. She was used to her mother changing her mind. Like about having another child when she'd seemed satisfied with only one. Emily slipped on her glasses. It was Mrs. Barrett, all right, fiddling with the strand of pearls swaying from her scrawny neck. She was wearing the same plain, tailored clothes she always wore—Best & Co. clothes, Emily now realized. She leaned against a table piled with pink and blue baby blankets set off by a display of marble hearts. They were just like the ones on Phoebe's dresser.

Instead of a marble heart, Phoebe had given Emily a plaid headband for her birthday.

"She must be buying a baby gift," Lady Lenore said.

"Uh-uh. She's waiting on that young pregnant woman." Emily emphasized the word "young." "Only that's weird, because Phoebe told me she does volunteer work tutoring poor children in a public school."

"Is that what Phoebe told you? She must have lied about where her mother works. Maybe she finds it embarrassing. For a society woman like her mother, volunteer work is expected, but if you work for a salary, you're supposed to have a job with more prestige than selling baby clothes."

"What's wrong with selling baby clothes?" It was better than buying them for your own baby when you were almost forty, Emily thought. But if there wasn't anything wrong with it, why would Phoebe lie? It made sense that her mother should be working for money, instead of volunteering, since her father had stopped teaching at Columbia to write his book.

"Society women don't have jobs like this. I stopped working when I married your father."

Since when was Lady Lenore a society woman? "That doesn't count—you were his secretary."

"For your information, secretarial work requires a lot of training. I had to learn how to take Gregg shorthand and touch type."

Emily's mother had been a secretary for only three weeks before her father asked her out on a date. He proposed a week later.

"Maybe we should get out of here before Phoebe's mother sees us," she said.

"But what about my dress for the dance?"

"We'll go to Fashions for Girls."

"Yippee!" Fashions, as everyone called it, was for teenagers and it carried more grown-up clothing.

Was her mother right? Was Phoebe ashamed of her mother's job? Should Emily tell Phoebe she had seen her? Once again Emily wondered why her mother wanted another child. When she was little, Emily had begged for a baby sister or brother because all her friends had at least one, but now she was doing fine all by herself.

After Grandma Anna died, Emily's mother had left her with Harriet most days. Emily couldn't remember many mother-daughter outings: two or three previous trips to Best's and one to Fashions. One to the Bronx Zoo with her father along when she was in second grade. Two to the Great Woods ice-skating rink when Melissa's mother couldn't take them. A sleepover in Emily's room at the hospital when she had her tonsils out. A visit to the orthodontist, which ended in tears when Emily refused to have braces. And her mother had come with her to her entrance exam and interview at Bromley last fall because a parent had to be interviewed, too. Would her mother spend more time with the new baby?

Emily had almost forgotten about a once-regular shared activity: the weekly "Wella treatment." Every Saturday morning, after Emily washed her hair, her mother would lather her head with a thick, gooey cream and snap on a special heated bathing cap. Emily would sit with the cap over her head for a full hour while the Wella cream tamed her frizz. "This will help get rid of that coarse, wiry texture," her smooth-haired mother explained. But for some reason the treatments stopped as soon as they moved to New York.

Another, more pleasant memory rushed back. Before *The Diary of Anne Frank,* there had been a Broadway musical. When Emily was eight, her mother took her to see *Where's Charley?* Like the rest of the audience, they clapped wildly when the star, Ray Bolger, belted out "Once in Love with Amy," and demanded encores. He sang it again and again. They ended up seeing the play two more times together. Maybe there would be another musical like that. Her mother could leave Eva Jane with that Fräulein person and she would take Emily to a matinee.

On the way out of the Lilliputian Bazaar, Lady Lenore ducked into the ladies' room. Bring pregnant seemed to make her have to pee every two minutes. Emily wandered over to the table with the marble hearts. Phoebe's mother was across the floor at the cash register, arranging for the Silver Cross pram to be charged and sent. There was no one in sight. The hearts had no price tags. They were obviously display props. They weren't for sale. Emily snatched a coral heart and stuffed it in her pocket under a wad of Kleenex.

Shoplifting, it was called. She, Emily Judith Winter, was a kleptomaniac. A criminal! Tingles raced up and down her spine. She was scared—the kind of scared that made her chew her cuticles and bite the nails on both index fingers. Was she old enough to be arrested? She still hadn't seen *Rebel Without a Cause,* but she knew from the article in *Photoplay* that James Dean was taken to the police station after Sal Mineo got killed in a drag race.

But she hadn't been caught any of those times in Great Woods when she and Melissa had helped themselves to packs of trading cards from the candy store around the corner from school. In third grade, a large apartment building was built and the candy store closed. Had it gone broke because of all the stealing? Emily had pledged to herself she would never shoplift again. But Best's was an enormous store, with zillions of customers. There was no chance it would go out of business if she helped herself to one little heart.

Emily patted her other coat pocket, the one with her wallet in it. Everyone knew that you had to watch out for your money at all times—the city was crawling with pickpockets. Just the other day, a twelfth grader had been "picked" on the Eighty-sixth Street Crosstown when she bent over to tie her shoe. But Emily's wallet was still there, right next to the stolen heart. Was she any better than a pickpocket?

Her mother was taking her good old time—probably powdering her nose or blotting her lipstick. But returning the marble heart would be too risky. Emily hadn't been caught taking it, but someone—Phoebe's mother, maybe—might see her putting it back.

Lady Lenore scuffled out, looking like the Goodyear Blimp.

"I swear, I think there's a future football player in there!" she said, kneading her belly with obvious delight.

Emily had no choice but to keep the heart, she told herself. She massaged it, safe and snug in her pocket. How smooth it felt, how luxurious. What a perfect paperweight it would make—but how could she keep it in the open?

She would call Phoebe as soon as she got home from Fashions. "My mother let me get a sheath!" She could hear herself saying. Maybe the dress wouldn't be a sheath exactly, but it wouldn't have smocking at the top or one of those little-girl sashes that tied around the waist.

She wouldn't tell Phoebe about the marble heart, though. If she did, Phoebe would know that Emily knew her mother was a saleslady in a department store. Maybe Lady Lenore was right, for once. Maybe Phoebe's mother's job was a shameful secret.

"Stand up straight, Emily! You're slouching like your father! Do you want to be a hunchback?" she said, as they stepped on the down escalator. Emily pulled her shoulders up and back. Anything unattractive came from the Winter side of the family: stooped shoulders, bushy hair, nearsighted eyes, and any bad habit you could think of. Smooth hair, perfect posture, and 20/20 vision belonged to her mother's family. Those traits had not been passed down to Emily. Would Eva Jane have more luck?

Emily reached for the heart.

"And why are your hands in your pocket? Don't tell me you've started biting your nails again!" Standing at the curb on Fifth Avenue, her mother raised her hand high. Her long, arched, coral nails poked at the sky. A cab snorted to a stop.

"Are we going to Fashions?" Emily asked.

Her mother doubled over, grimacing fiercely. "We better get home. I think I'm in labor."

7 ❀ Diapers

"Fräulein, the pacifiers are burning!" Emily yelled as she turned the key in the front door lock. She tossed her coat on the foyer settee. She would keep her promise to hang it in the coat closet another time. Couldn't the baby nurse remember just once to turn off the burner before the whole house reeked of scorched rubber?

"Patience, *bitte!* The commercial will be on in one second!" Fräulein shouted from the nursery, where a rocking chair now occupied a permanent place in front of the small television set on which Emily used to watch *Dragnet.*

Fräulein left the television blaring and shuffled into the kitchen in her starched white uniform, her Brillo-textured orange hair wisping from under a cabbage-shaped nurse's cap. Emily wasn't sure how old she was. Over forty, but under sixty, was her guess.

"*Gott* forbid that Harriet should take a second to shut off the burner under the pacifiers while she cooks . . ." Fräulein muttered, pronouncing "while" like "vile." She doused the pot of pacifiers under cold water.

The kitchen had been turned into a laboratory. Cans of Carnation powdered milk, measuring cups filled with corn syrup and a sterilizer cluttered the counter. Pots brimming with rubber nipples and pacifiers simmered on the stove.

Emily had been watching television with Harriet on December 19, just three weeks before, on the eve of the day she had hoped to see *Rebel Without a Cause* with Phoebe, while her mother took all night to give birth. At 5:27 in the morning, just as Emily was nodding off, Lord Sidney called up with the news. Evan Joel Winter had arrived, weighing in at eight pounds, ten ounces. Because he was so humongous, Lady Lenore had to have a Caesarian section. She had stitches all the way up her stomach and had to stay at Lying-In Hospital for two whole weeks. Injections for pain made her sleepier than Evan. You couldn't hear him cry through the hospital nursery windows, but whenever Emily visited he was awake, with his mouth wide open in what she assumed was a howl.

Emily didn't mind that Evan had come home, but Fräulein was another matter. Signs of her invasion were everywhere. She had taken over the bathroom too. Two bottles of Roux hair dye, a package of hairpins, a hairnet, a jar of mineral oil, and Orange Flame lipstick and matching nail polish crowded the medicine cabinet. The closet in Evan's room, where Emily had thrown old board games and sports equipment, now held three white uniforms, two white cardigans, and a puffy muskrat coat.

"I won't touch that there equipment," Harriet was saying. "My mama fed me from her bosoms, like woman was born to do."

Emily sided with Harriet. She didn't see why other people should be doing Fräulein's job. And wasn't some of it Lady Lenore's job, too?

She didn't completely fault her mother, though. What was interesting about a formless creature who didn't even grasp your finger the way infants were supposed to? She nicknamed Evan the Blob. Come to think of it, maybe there was something wrong with him.

"My *Mutti* gave me and my sisters her milk, too," Fräulein said, pointing to her chest, as if her own drooping breasts had been the source. She offered Harriet a conciliatory gumdrop. "If only that were a guarantee for a long and healthy life!"

Did she mean that her sisters were dead? Fräulein had already alluded to a disaster in her past. Could she have hidden in an attic, like Anne Frank? Had her sisters been in a concentration camp? Emily refused to give her the satisfaction of asking.

Fräulein cocked her head toward the nursery. "Ah, the commercial is over! Please, *Gott*, the audience should vote for this poor woman to get a collie for her little girl! She said she wants a dog just like Lassie, but she has trouble talking because of a tumor in her brain."

Fräulein rarely missed *Queen for a Day,* on which a housewife with a pile of troubles was granted her fondest wish. She watched the evening quiz shows, too—*The Big Surprise* and especially *The $64,000 Question.* She was in awe of Dr. Joyce Brothers, a psychologist who had won the top prize for knowing everything there was to know about boxing.

Over dinner the night before, her mouth stuffed with seconds or thirds of Harriet's chicken breaded with crushed cornflakes, Fräulein raved about the current contestant, a plumber who was an expert on Jane Austen.

"And he didn't even finish high school!" she said.

I'm not going to finish high school, either, if I have to have dinner with you every night, Emily thought.

"Doesn't the noise keep Evan up?" her mother asked.

"It is a mistake to be silent around babies, always shushing. They should learn how to sleep through everything," Fräulein had said.

Now she spun around now to face Emily. "Where were you, young lady, may I ask?"

No, you may not, Emily was tempted to say. What gave Fräulein the right? She was in charge of the Blob, not her. But would it kill her to answer? "Over at Alice Unger's," Emily said.

Harriet clasped her hands to her cheeks. "Lordy me, *there's* an unhappy child!"

"*Jawohl,*" Fräulein agreed.

"How would *you* know?" Emily asked. Harriet and Fräulein were prying busybodies, both of them.

"Laundry room chit-chat," Harriet said, waggling her chapped knuckles. "They say that grouchy mother of hers got the polio when she was expecting Alice, so she blames her and picks on the poor girl all the time." So Alice was right. Did Fräulein and Harriet gossip about Emily in the laundry room, too?

"I better check on Master Evan," Fräulein said. Check on the next quiz show is more like it, Emily thought, as Fräulein rushed off to the nursery. Fortunately for her, the Blob did a fair amount of sleeping, even if he woke up for a bottle in the middle of the night.

At the other end of the apartment, Emily found her mother stretched out on the chaise longue in her bedroom, wearing a silky bed jacket. She removed a silver rattle from a robin's-egg blue box. "I'll have to get this monogrammed," she said. As if Evan would care whether a rattle had his initials on it or not!

Her mother handed her an elaborately wrapped package. "How nice of Aunt Irene to think of you!"

Emily tore the gift wrapping off *The Secret of the Old Clock,* a Nancy Drew mystery. She had read all the Nancy Drews and even the Cherry Ames nurse books and the Vicki Barr stewardess books by fourth grade. Even if Aunt Irene wasn't a real aunt, she should remember how old Emily was.

"I don't read baby books, in case she's interested," Emily said.

"I think it was extremely thoughtful of her," her mother said. "You'll have to send a thank you note."

Fräulein came in with Evan, who was working up to a full-blown scream. She handed him to Lady Lenore. "I thought you might want to try the four o'clock feeding today."

"I don't think I'm ready yet, Fräulein. The incision still throbs. And what if he spits up?" Lady Lenore said, handing Evan back awkwardly. "I'm afraid I was never good with baby messes."

That was putting it mildly. Emily's mother had always been a neatness and cleanliness freak. She would never forget that time at Melissa's sixth birthday party. Like all the other girls, Emily had been dressed in party clothes—a pink smocked dress and frilly ankle socks with white Mary Janes.

She'd gotten fidgety, sitting on the miniature folding chairs to watch the hired clown, so she and Melissa escaped to the backyard to practice cartwheels. It had been raining. Within seconds their party dresses were coated with mud.

As Melissa's mother dabbed at her dress with a soapy rag, Emily couldn't stop crying. "My mother will have a fit."

"Oh, no, I'm sure she won't mind!" Melissa's mother said. "It's only dirt. It'll come out in the washing machine."

When her mother pulled up in her perfectly polished maroon convertible, Emily was shaking. "You really are worried, aren't you?" Melissa's mother said with disbelief. She ran up to the car. "The girls got mud on their clothes playing in the backyard. I told Emily you'd understand."

"Of course," Emily's mother said, forcing a smile. But in the car she had yelled at Emily. Nowadays she yelled at Emily for not hanging up her coat. She yelled at Lord Sidney for dropping dirty socks and cigar ashes on the floor. Ever since she'd discovered a dried noodle stuck to the bottom of a casserole, she insisted on checking the pots and pans after Harriet scrubbed them.

"How did I, of all people, end up in a family of slobs?" she liked to say. And now there was the Blob, the biggest slob of all.

So it was not surprising that it was Fräulein who fed Evan, walked him up and down when he screamed, rubbed his back to make him burp, mopped up smelly spit-ups and poops, safety pinned diapers and pulled rubber pants over his froglike thighs and sponged him in a large rubber contraption called a bathinette, which was not the same thing as the bassinette, the fancy wicker cot he slept in. Whenever possible, her eyes stayed glued to the television screen.

Alice was the only friend who stopped by to take a peek at the Blob, if only to see how blobby he was. Phoebe, who had often told Emily she was lucky not to be an only child any longer, stayed away. Melissa had promised to take the train in on a weekend, but so far she hadn't.

"I have an idea!" Fräulein said, filling a baby bottle and

screwing on a freshly sterilized nipple. "Maybe Emily is vanting to learn how to give her brother his formula."

I am not vanting to learn how to give my brother his formula, Emily wanted to say. Then again, anything was more fun than solving algebra equations.

"Good idea!" her mother said. "But make sure she does it correctly."

This was probably part of the let-her-help-out ruse, but still, Emily followed Fräulein into the nursery.

On television, an elderly woman with almost no teeth was pleading for money to pay for repairs on her trailer.

"This case will surely go to the 'heart line,'" Fräulein predicted, gently placing Evan in Emily's arms.

The heart line? Emily had a sudden urge to check her bottom desk drawer, where the marble heart, still swaddled in Kleenex, was tucked in the corner behind her comic book collection, but how could she, with the Blob in her arms?

How cozy he looked! Lulled by the glup-glup of his sucking after she placed the nipple in his mouth, Emily watched the trailer lady weep with joy as a wealthy couple phoned the "heart line" to offer her a room in a shack on their estate, as well as money for dentures.

"So there are some decent people in the world," Fräulein muttered with a deep sigh. "Like your Sergeant Friday. He is, how you say, an amazing guy."

"You watch *Dragnet*?" Emily asked. It was her favorite program, but she hadn't watched it since Evan was born.

"I watched for the first time last week, but I am already, how you say, a fan. It starts at eight o'clock, no? In four hours, just when Evan's next feeding is scheduled."

When Emily returned to the nursery at feeding time, the television was already tuned to Channel 4.

"Dum-de-dum-dum," she hummed with Fräulein as the program's jingle came on, followed by Sgt. Joe Friday's voice: "The story you are about to see is true. The names have been changed to protect the innocent. This is the city: Los Angeles, California."

Los Angeles looked a little like Great Woods, but with palm trees, Emily always thought.

"It was 9:15 a.m. and we were working the morning shift out of robbery," Sergeant Friday intoned in a gravelly monotone.

A grocery clerk had gone missing. "This is the first time he's spent a night away from me," his wife said, opening the door to her bungalow in a housecoat and curlers. "He suffers from insomnia and——"

"Just the facts, ma'am," Sergeant Friday interrupted. Minutes later, he found her husband, bound and gagged in his car with his wallet stolen. Sergeant Friday caught the mugger, too.

Sergeant Friday always found the crook. For him, right and wrong were never mixed up. Phony alibis were always exposed. The guilty didn't stand a chance. If someone like Sergeant Friday had caught Emily that day at Best's, she'd be in a jail for juvenile delinquents.

Instead, she was safe and sound at home watching television with her brother's baby nurse.

"Next time we will learn how to burp, *ja?*" Fräulein picked Evan up and carried him to the changing table. "Babies swallow air, which gives them gas." She pronounced the word "which" as "vitch."

Not on your life, Emily thought, though she had a hunch she'd be back.

8 ❀ Shining Armor

"When are we going to play Avalon?" Alice shouted into the phone. It was the next-to-last day of vacation. Avalon was a game Emily and Phoebe had invented, in which Central Park was the forest where the knight Tristan met in secret with his beloved Isolde. Emily didn't think Alice would enjoy the game as much.

"We can do it today."

"We don't need costumes, do we?"

"Of course not," Emily said.

They didn't need props, either. But when they met in front of the building, Alice pulled a silver baby cup from her pocket. "I thought this would be good for the fatal love potion."

"We're nowhere near the last scene yet," Emily said.

With the temperature just above freezing, the Eighty-sixth Street entrance to the park was deserted. Trees rattled their brittle branches. Flapping their wings, jittery pigeons grunted at the feet of an old woman in a tattered coat, who was sowing bread crumbs. On the bridle path, a man in a ski parka and jodhpurs cantered by on a chestnut horse.

When he had passed, Emily scaled a mound of low rocks, proclaiming: "Oh, Tristan, thou art the boldest knight in all the kingdom!" She gripped her throat. "But what if your liege finds out about us?"

"So what if he does?" Alice said. "There's no one to play my liege, anyway."

She was no substitute for Phoebe, that was clear. "Come

on, you're supposed to say something like, 'Forsooth, he shall behead me! But I will ply my love beyond the grave!'" Emily said.

"Forsooth, he shall behead me!" Alice repeated without enthusiasm. "This is idiotic. Now it's my turn to be Isolde!"

"Now it's my turn to be Isolde," repeated a croaky male voice nearby.

"Prithee, damsel in distress, here cometh your knight in shining armor to the rescue!" echoed another.

"Never fear, Tristan is here!" A deeper voice called out.

A bunch of boys wearing dark green Kensington varsity jackets emerged from behind a jagged cluster of rocks. Ted from dancing school was one of them. Emily could make out the scar on his cheek, even at a distance. She felt herself turn as pink as the stick of Bazooka in her pocket.

This was far more embarrassing than the time she and Phoebe had bumped into Miss Lockwood in the Armor Room at the Metropolitan Museum. The girls had been trying to picture how knights looked inside their suits of armor while Miss Lockwood was doing research for her Ph.D. dissertation.

"Ah, what I love to see: Bromley girls carrying their studies into their leisure activities," she said. "Allow me to point out that these are later examples of armor. Earlier knights weren't dressed as dashingly, as it were. Nor were they as well protected. They wore only chain mail." Claiming they had to meet somebody, the girls had fled to the Egyptian Wing.

This time Emily fled behind a tree.

"Ready to chug-a-lug the love potion?" a boy with a peeling tan asked. He pointed to the silver cup Alice still held in her gloved hand.

Crouching, Emily wrapped her Princeton scarf around her face, mummy-style.

"Not yet," Alice said. "We're rehearsing a play, and in this scene Isolde has to try to find Tristan, who's being pursued by enemy hordes."

Alice was a quick thinker, Emily had to admit.

"Oh, yeah? Here we come, ready or not!" the boys said.

Emily's scarf slipped away just in time for her to see the boy she had met at Flora Freund's standing inches in front of her.

"Tristan, I presume?" said the boy with a peeling tan.

Tristan! Emily had never been more mortified. How would she ever live this down?

"At B-Bromley, girls play the boys' parts," she stammered.

Maybe Ted wouldn't recognize her with her glasses on— she never wore them to dancing school.

But he recognized her, all right. "Hi—Emily, right?" he said.

"Hi, Ted," she squeaked. Her mouth was frozen; she could barely open it.

Ted looked surprised. "Have I had the pleasure, Tristan?" asked the boy with the tan, looking directly at her.

"Is your name Ted, too?" Emily asked. It was a pretty common name.

"Vamoose," said another boy. "Let's get the hell away from these weirdos."

"That's why we call it Broomley—because of the witches who go there!" said another boy.

Ted—but was he Ted?—cast an apologetic backward glance as the group galumphed away, chanting, "Broomley's for witches. Bromley girls are bitches!"

"I've never been so humiliated in my life," Emily said. "One of those boys was the one I want to invite to the class dance."

"How do you think I feel? You and your babyish games! I'll be the laughingstock of Kensington!" Alice said, trying to catch her breath as they ran toward Park Avenue.

"You agreed to play!" Besides, Alice didn't know any Kensington boys. She didn't go to dancing school.

"We're too old to 'play!' I was just trying to be nice. Which one was Ted, *the* Ted, anyway? Because the boy with the peeling skin seemed to be named, Ted, too."

"The one with the scar."

Alice gasped. "Of course! How could I not notice him? He has eyebrows that touch."

Emily ignored the comment. "How can I go back to Flora Freund's?"

"So don't go back! You don't like Flora Freund's, anyway."

"My mother will have a fit if I don't."

"Why tell her? Pretend you're going, but come over to my house every other Friday night. Your mother doesn't know I don't go to dancing school, does she? Leave your house wearing your party stuff and tell her we're taking a cab together. You can keep a change of clothes in my closet. Then make sure to dress up again and go home at the right time," Alice said, unlocking her front door.

"How come you don't have to go?" Emily asked.

"Since we're not that Jewish, my parents don't approve of a dancing school that's only for Jews."

"But you don't have a choice. Miss Thornberry's, the dancing school Cressida and Phoebe go to, would never accept you," Emily said.

"I think you have a persecution complex! Just because Phoebe isn't friends with you anymore doesn't mean it's because you're Jewish. Cressida and company are cliquey, that's all. I had my own clique in fourth grade. Barbara Kaplan, Gail Roth, and me."

"The Jewish girls."

"Pure coincidence! Anyway, I'm not friends with them anymore."

Alice dragged Emily over to where the framed St. Charles certificate hung over a desk in the living room. It showed a sketch of a clipper ship and several columns of signatures with S-shaped Fs like in the Declaration of Independence. "See, there it is—Hendricks—that was my great-great-great-great grandfather. He was kind of a pilgrim."

"But he was still Jewish," Emily said.

"I'm tired of talking about who's Jewish and who's not. Bettina has tons of friends who aren't Jewish. Kit, her boyfriend, isn't Jewish."

That only reminded Emily of her biggest worry: Did she dare invite Ted to the class dance?

Anyway, was Ted his name? Were there two Teds?

She had planned to call him tonight, but after what happened, it was out of the question. She would have to put it off a while longer. Maybe he would forget what had happened in the park.

9 ❀ Taffeta

Gripping the stolen marble heart for good luck, Emily dragged a step stool across the linoleum to the phone on the kitchen pantry wall. It had been a week since the Avalon encounter, and, even though she still shuddered at the thought of that disaster, the class dance was only a month away and she couldn't put off calling Ted any longer.

Next to her on the counter a fresh supply of nipples and pacifiers stewed in the autoclave, a new kind of sterilizer that turned on and off automatically. She hoped the noise wouldn't be heard at the other end of the phone.

She had a whopper of a cold—not that anyone noticed. After dinner, on the way to the theater, Lady Lenore had floated by her desk, a cloud of taffeta and Arpège, the perfume she always wore, without so much as a God bless you when Emily sneezed—one of those sneezes where you can't catch the snot in time. At dinner, no one commented when she had a coughing fit while Fräulein raved about a new quiz show contestant, a retired typing teacher who was an authority on Shakespeare. How could her mother, the neatness fiend, not have complained about the pile of crumpled tissues on the desk?

It was just as well she didn't suggest Emily see Dr. Lieberman, the new pediatrician. At her fall checkup, he'd barely grumbled hello before trailing the chilly metal stethoscope over her chest. She'd almost gagged when he shoved the tongue depressor way down her throat. And when she had a fever over Thanksgiving, he woke her from a nap with his house call.

"I'm an unknown, a human X," Emily thought, as she blotted a glob of snot off a sheet of algebra equations. She placed a
box of Kleenex and a glass of water on the counter. She didn't
want to cough and sneeze when she spoke to Ted. She spread
the script she and Phoebe had worked on across her quaking
knees. She'd added to it. Beads of sweat clumped under her
bangs. The butterflies in her stomach were doing high dives.
She read the script out loud one more time. The cold had made
her hoarse; her voice was lower than usual.

Emily: Hello, Mrs. Margolin?

Mrs. M.: Why, yes. Who's calling, please?

Emily: It's Emily Winter. Is Ted home?

[Brief pause]
Mrs. M.: I'll go see.
[Sound of footsteps echoing down a long corridor]

Ted: Hi, Emily. How's tricks?

Emily: I'm fine. Didn't you think the punch was icky at Flora
    Freund's last time? [Or, Wasn't Flora a sight in that violet
    gown?]

Ted: Yes, but I liked the waltz, didn't you?

Emily: Me, too. They'll be playing some waltzes at our class
    dance and I thought maybe you'd like to come. It's at
    Bromley on Friday, January 11th. [Or did that sound too
    old-fashioned, like something from a book by Jane Aus-
    ten?]

Ted: [She crossed out "Why, yes."] Sure, I'd love to!

Emily (coolly): Good. [Now for a topic of conversation!!!!] Did
    you see *The Court Jester* yet? [She'd decided to take Phoe-
    be's advice, after all.]

Ted (enthusiastically): Of course! "The pellet with the poisle is
    in the flaggle with the chalice," and all those other tongue
    twisters.

Next came a section Emily hadn't cleared with Phoebe, which she had scribbled on the bottom of the page. She knew that Ted wasn't likely to say this, but still . . .

Ted: Can you keep a secret? I didn't really like *The Court Jester.*

Emily: Neither did I!

Ted: Now *Rebel Without a Cause*—there's a movie I'd like to see!

Emily: "Me too, I'm dying to see it!"

[And then, maybe, just maybe, he'd suggest they see it together.]

Emily's hands shook as she dialed Ted's number, which she'd gotten from Flora Freund's office. Maybe the line would be busy. Maybe it would be busy for so long she'd have to try again another time. Part of her wished that would happen.

A deep voice answered after half a ring. "Hello?"

"Uh, hi, it's Emily Winter."

"Hey, Gruber, you son of a bitch! Resorting to sounding like a girl—too much! Have you no decency?"

The marble heart rolled out of Emily's hand and crashed to the floor.

"Gruber? 'Tis you, is it not?"

"Uh, no. It's me. Emily Winter." Had her voice really sounded that deep?

Silence followed—the creepy kind.

"From Flora Freund's?" Emily stared at the marble heart, which lay in pieces on the floor.

"Hey, my profoundest apologies. This jerk in my class, my dear friend from forever and practical joker extraordinaire, Rob Gruber, just hung up on me while discussing a matter of extreme importance and I thought he was calling back to express deepest regrets."

The trouble with a one-sided script was that the other side didn't know any of the lines. Emily's mouth clamped shut.

"You say you met me at old Froggy Farts?" Ted prompted. "Pardon my French—I mean, Flora Freund's."

This boy certainly didn't sound like the person she had met at dancing school. He sounded like the boy who had answered to Ted that day in the park.

And the other boy, the one with the scar, was named Rob.

"Yes, we were doing the waltz," Emily managed. Her mouth was dry as a beach.

"Over my dead body! That dance should be outlawed. When they strike up *The Blue Danube,* I seek refuge in the little boys' room. If I'm going to be dizzy, I'd rather do it raiding the pater's liquor cabinet. You must have somebody else in mind. A classical case of mistaken identity, I fear."

Maybe she could just hang up, Emily thought. But the real Ted was still talking. "You know, I bet it was one of old Gruber's tricks! I wouldn't put it past him. He goes to Froggy's, too. You can't miss him—he's the knave with the dueling scar."

For some reason, the boy with the scar—was it really from a duel?—had used Ted's name when they had danced together just before vacation.

Emily tried to reconstruct that last class at Flora Freund's. It had started with the usual Paul Jones round. When the music stopped, Emily landed on the boy with the scar. He told her his name was Ted Margolin. He'd said he loved the waltz.

"The boy I danced with did have a scar," Emily said.

"He still does! Well, now that I think we've solved the mystery, how can I be of assistance, oh, damsel of enigma?"

Emily forced her mouth open. "I thought I was calling to invite you to our class dance. But I guess I met this Rob Gruber, not you." Before she knew it, she heard herself say, "It's at Bromley on Friday night, January 11th. Can you come?"

"At Bromley, you say? You wouldn't happen to know some girls there who are putting on a play about Tristan and Isolde? They were rehearsing in the park. One of them spoke to Rob. Come to think of it, her name was Emily."

"N-n-no," Emily said. She felt faint.

"Never mind, then. Your invitation is not entirely displeasing. Trouble is, I have this girlfriend—*une amie,* shall we say—in the ninth grade at Chatham. I don't think she'd take kindly to my dancing at Bromley."

"I guess not." Emily crumpled the script like a sheet of old math proofs. It landed next to the jagged marble chunks strewn across the floor.

"But *merci beaucoup,* my dear. I'm going to have to have a word with the old Robber. Be sure to identify yourself next week at Froggy's! Adieu!"

Click. Emily heard his receiver drop back into the cradle. There would be no next week at Flora Freund's, she decided. She was never going again. But she would be back at Bromley, and she had to know who her date would be in time for a special homeroom meeting about the class dance scheduled for the first day after vacation.

She had to speak to somebody. She dialed Melissa. She still knew her number by heart: GW-9-5547. The line was busy.

On the sixth try, Melissa finally picked up.

"Who's this?"

"Emily—Emily Winter."

Melissa hadn't recognized her voice because of her cold, Emily told herself.

"Emily, gee, how's tricks?"

"Great. And you?"

"Terrific! Ninth grade is the best! The best teachers, the best sports teams, even yummy food. And, best of all, I have a boyfriend!"

"Lucky you!" Emily felt her heart sink, as if it, too, were made of marble.

"It's kind of like we're going steady."

Emily's heart sank another few degrees. "Is he from school?"

"No, I met him at my cousin's bar mitzvah. His name is Mark Stern and he's a sophomore at Great Meadows High." Great Meadows was the next town over. "We're going to see *Rebel Without a Cause* together this weekend."

"Lucky stiff!" Emily felt a lump make its way up her throat.

"I guess it's hard meeting boys when you go to a girls' school," Melissa said. Her pitying tone annoyed Emily.

"Oh, it's a cinch. There are all these hangouts—this great pizza parlor and these soda shops——"

"Emily, I really want to catch up, I do," Melissa interrupted, "but Mark is supposed to call any minute and I don't want him to get a busy signal."

"Bye!" Emily said as the lump turned into tears.

"I'll call you back soon, Em, promise, hope to die!"

As the tears rolled down her cheeks, Emily realized she had no choice but to invite Davy. He had come to all her birthday parties. He was at Melissa's, the time they fell in the mud. Emily had pictures of him in disguise, wearing cowboy hats and pirates' bandannas and even a surgeon's mask. Like Rob Gruber, whoever he was—like so many people, it seemed—Davy liked to pretend he was someone else.

But Davy wasn't a *boy* boy. Phoebe had said that Emily's relationship with him was "strictly platonic." Certainly, they had never kissed on the lips. Davy made Emily think of Great Woods—of the split-level house with the converted basement, the swing set nobody used, and the kitchen with the first Disposall ever. You could throw down any garbage except chicken bones. No one in Manhattan had a Disposall. At 1163 Park, bare-chested maintenance workers heaved the garbage down fiery incinerators.

"Hi, Davy!" Emily said, when he picked up the phone. She hadn't spoken to him since she'd moved to the city.

"Oy'm afraid you have de wraw-ung numbah," Davy said, in what must have been his idea of a Long Island accent. "Dis is Noo Yawk Bug-Awf Exterminators and deah's no Davy heah."

He had once called pretending to be the manager of the RKO Palace in Manhasset. "Miss Emily Winter? I found your wallet," he'd said in a businesslike voice. He knew that she'd lost it, but what he didn't know was that the real manager had already called to say he had found it. Anyway, Davy's voice hadn't been low enough. It was lower now, Emily noticed.

"I have a job for you," she said. She was willing to play along for a minute.

"You need me to get rid of some pests at that new school of yours?" he asked. He had dropped the accent.

Emily took a deep breath. "Can you come to my class dance?"

"Are boys allowed?"

"It's the only time they can set foot in the school," she said.

"Okay, I'll set foot. I guess my parents can drive me in."

Almost immediately Emily regretted having invited him. Behind his back, everyone called him Drippy Davy. How would he fit in? Maybe she should call him back in a week and tell him the dance was canceled because of a fire in the auditorium or because a student's mother, or maybe the student herself—how about Cressida?—had just died of a fatal disease.

Just then, noisy applause erupted from Evan's room. On *The $64,000 Question,* the Shakespeare expert had won again. But she, Emily, was a loser. So was Davy, for that matter. He had skipped kindergarten but he wasn't as brainy as he thought. He liked to brag about the time he was a Whiz Kid on the radio but left out the minor detail about losing in the first round.

What if he tried to kiss her? Did he even know how? Would he remove his eyeglasses? Movie stars didn't kiss with glasses on. But Davy never took his off. He taped them to his temples when he went swimming in the Great Woods municipal pool. "If a shark comes along, I should be able to see it!" he joked.

Emily needed practice, just in case. She reached up to the top shelf of her closet for the glossy foldout of Laurence Olivier, which Phoebe and she shared, the one they had ordered from a fan club in England. Emily had airmailed a ten-dollar bill and the head shot arrived three weeks later. Until Thanksgiving, they'd traded it back and forth—one week, Phoebe had it to herself, the next it was Emily's. Emily had it for Thanksgiving and Phoebe hadn't asked for it since.

She smoothed out the picture and taped it to her bedroom door. From an article in *Silver Screen,* she knew that Laurence Olivier was exactly 5' 10½". Measuring up from the floor with a yardstick, drawing little pencil marks every 12 inches, she calculated where his head would reach. Of course, this measurement could not be exact because, in real life, he would swoop down as he did with Merle Oberon in *Wuthering Heights* or, in private, with his wife Vivien Leigh, and scoop her in his arms. But ninth-grade boys probably didn't kiss like movie stars.

Craning upward, Emily searched for the cleft in his chin. In a hurry to hide the picture from her mother one day, she had folded it in quarters. A whole row of clefts now rippled across L.O.'s cheeks and chin.

Trying to ignore them, Emily stood on tiptoe, twisted her mouth to one side, and pressed her lips to his. No real boy would ever kiss her, she thought. She'd be stuck kissing pictures of movie stars forever.

The door opened, almost toppling her.

"Ach! I used to do the same thing," Fräulein said. Her broad grin exposed the shiny gold fillings in her back teeth. "I stood on a stool practicing to kiss the principal of our school! I had clipped a picture from the newspaper. He was so handsome, so *schön,* just like a star from your Hollywood!"

"Ever heard of privacy?" Emily said, ripping the photo off the door.

"I beg your apologies. I was only coming to get you because *Dragnet* is about to begin."

"I know when *Dragnet* is on," Emily snapped. Fräulein had some nerve coming in without knocking, but at least her intentions were good. Watching *Dragnet* would cheer her up, Emily thought. She followed Fräulein into the nursery.

"First, a word from our sponsor," said a wavy-haired brunette. She held up a pack of Chesterfields, the brand Sergeant

Friday himself smoked. "Put a smile in your smoking," she said, lifting a cigarette to her ruby red lips.

Just then Emily remembered the shattered heart. She ran back to the kitchen. She gathered the broken pieces in a paper bag and stuffed it in her desk drawer. Maybe they could be glued together.

"I don't want to go to our class dance!" she said when she returned to the nursery.

"Ach, Emily!" Fräulein patted her on the back as if to bring up a burp. "It is something with the boys, *ja?*"

On the screen, Sergeant Friday was conferring with his assistant. Fräulein turned down the volume. "Emily, *liebchen,* you are thinking the boys are so suave, so debonair, like our Mister Friday here? They are shy, like you. You are all, boys and girls, at this time of life—how you are calling it?—the middle age."

Emily couldn't help giggling. Fräulein's broken English made her come up with the most absurd things. "You're thinking of the Middle Ages, the period we're studying in history—knights and ladies and the feudal system. The stage of life you're talking about is the teens. I have no idea how you say teenager in German." In other languages, it occurred to Emily, numbers did not end in "teen."

"But this stage, it is smack in the middle," Fräulein insisted. "Not of life—but of the way you think. You are between child and grown-up, a mixture of girl and woman."

She was making her sound like some kind of freak, Emily thought. As if to protest, Evan grunted in his sleep.

"Well, it's very complicated, but this boy I invited to the dance—Ted—he wasn't the one I thought I was inviting," Emily said.

"The boys of fourteen and fifteen, they are so immature! It is easy to get them mixed up. They all have the same pimples."

It was no use. Fräulein just didn't get it. "This trouble—it should be the worst thing that ever happens to you," she said.

"Right now, it is!" Emily stormed out of the room. Once again, Fräulein was alluding to a tragedy and aftermath of her own, against which other people's problems paled.

"Come back, Emily," Fräulein said gently. "Now is when our favorite detective finds out the truth."

Emily was still angry, but how could she not stay for the end?

Sergeant Friday was knocking on the door of a rundown bungalow. A man in an undershirt who had an anchor tattooed down his biceps opened the door a crack. "I know the law," he said, running his fingers through his pomaded hair.

"So why'd you break it?" Sergeant Friday snarled. He snapped a pair of handcuffs around the man's wrists.

Fräulein turned off the sound. "During the war, people didn't bother to knock when they dragged you from your home. That handsome principal and his family were taken to a concentration camp. Have you heard of this kind of camp, where they gas you or starve you to death?" Fräulein's whole body began to shake. "It is not like your American summer camps, with the swimming lessons and the hiking and this thing called color war."

Emily gulped. "I think Anne Frank died in a concentration camp."

"Anne Frank and six million other people. She wasn't the only one to kiss her boyfriend for the last time."

Though it was hard to imagine, with her web of wrinkles and her carroty hair and her orange lipstick pooling in the corners of her mouth, Emily realized that Fräulein had once been a teenager like herself, with crushes and best friends.

"But I consider myself one of the lucky ones," Fräulein said. "Here I am, in the United States of America, where criminals are caught and there is no hating of Jews!"

Fräulein thought she was an authority on everything, but clearly Emily had to set her straight.

"Oh, yeah? It so happens that some girls at Bromley have been picking on the Jewish girls. I think my friend Phoebe is one of them. She avoids me. She never comes over anymore. She didn't even visit after Evan was born."

"This cannot be true!" Fräulein said. "Not in a country where a Jewess like Joyce Brothers can win $64,000 on television!" Before the plumber and the typing teacher, Joyce Brothers had been her favorite quiz show contestant.

"Oh, it's true, all right." Emily told her what she and Alice had overheard at the Peachtree. When she came to the part about how everyone, including Phoebe, had joined the Anti–Clothes Girl League, Fräulein clapped her hands over her ears.

"So that Phoebe is not a friend, after all. I have wondered why the only girl I met is this poor Alice who you don't seem to care for so very much," she said.

Oblivious to their raised voices, Evan had drifted off. Fräulein wound his powder blue monogrammed blanket snugly around him. Her upper arms swung like hammocks from the short sleeves of her nylon uniform as she lowered him into the bassinette.

"When I was your age, my friends and I went over to each other's houses every day after school. We gobbled homebaked *apfelkuchen* and dressed up in our *Muttis'* clothes to put on plays," she said wistfully.

"Bully for you." Emily still found it hard to imagine Fräulein as a teenager.

"It didn't turn out so well. Those friends are no longer with us."

Did she mean they had all been killed in concentration camps? Instinctively, Emily put her hand over Fräulein's. Was she actually trying to comfort her? She pulled her hand back. Sad things had happened to Fräulein, but that didn't give her the right to be a gossip and a busybody. Emily reminded herself that she couldn't wait for Evan to give up his night bottle and sleep through the night so that Fräulein could leave.

"I love feeding infants—they have such hearty appetites," Fräulein continued. "But after my babies gain enough weight to sleep through the night, I move on to the next case, just like Sergeant Friday." She slapped her hands together dismissively. "That way I don't become too attached. You must never let yourself become too attached."

"But I miss Phoebe," Emily said. She was tempted to tell Fräulein about Phoebe's diet, but she had told her more than enough already.

"Of course you do," Fräulein said. "But she should never have joined that group."

She turned up the volume as soon as Sergeant Friday appeared on screen again. "Let us now hear how the criminal will be punished!" she said, raising a finger to her orange lips.

She shook her head in disbelief as the thief was sentenced to three to five years in the Los Angeles County Jail.

"He deserves more! Your classmates—they should be punished too! Hating Jews must not be allowed! Not in New York! Not in America! You must speak up to those girls!"

"I know," Emily whispered. Fräulein was right. She should tell them off and someday she thought she would. But right now she longed to be one of them.

10 ❀ A Dress Code

Careful not to smudge Miss Lockwood's column of "Nifty New Words," Cressida marked off three columns on the blackboard. She headed the first, "Girls," the second "Dates," and the third, "Stags."

"This is to list our dates and stags with the schools they go to," Cressida instructed. In the square block letters Bromley girls were taught to write with instead of cursive script, she printed her name at the top of the first column and wrote in large letters under "Dates":

Player Crosby   Harvard

"Swoon, swoon!" Margery said, clutching her throat. "He's the dreamiest!"

"Some girls have all the luck," Eugenia said, her voice dripping with envy.

"Is Player his real name?" Emily asked.

"Yes, believe it or not," Alice said. "But doesn't he still go to Kensington?"

"Yeah, isn't he in eleventh grade?" asked Lindsley.

"It just so happens he was able to skip his senior year because of his college board scores and the advanced courses he took last year, and, when he was six, they made him skip second grade because he was reading books like *Gulliver's Travels*," Cressida said. "That's why he's already a freshman at Harvard."

She picked up a fresh piece of chalk and moved over to the "Stags" column. She wrote:

Timothy Jessup, Jr.	Kensington
Nathaniel Bradford	Greening School for Boys
Terence Mackay III	Oldover Academy
Connor Craig	St. Wenceslas Priory
Rob Gruber	Kensington

Emily wasn't sure what a stag was but apparently Rob Gruber, alias Ted Margolin, was one of them. Before she could stop herself, she blurted out, "What exactly's a stag?" Cressida threw her a look of pure scorn, ordering, "No one tell her! If she's so smart, she'll figure it out all by herself." Which she would have, if she'd stopped to think for even a second.

"A male deer!" Margery shouted with a mocking whoop.

"They're extra boys, Em," Alice whispered. "They cut in on Cressida, or maybe Margery, now that she's so busty. But mostly they just stand around, looking bored."

Why was Rob one of Cressida's extras? How did she even know him? She had so many others—did she have to list him, too? At least that meant he would probably come to the dance.

Holly ran up to the blackboard. "But Rob goes to Flora Freund's!" She mouthed in Cressida's ear, loud enough for Emily to hear.

"So?"

"So what about the League rules? I thought we're not allowed to have anything to do with, uh, Flora Freund people."

"Shush! That only goes for the *girls,* you lamebrain! Extra boys are always welcome."

"Sorry if I'm not a mind reader," said Holly.

Don't just sit there, Emily told herself. Speak up! But what exactly would she say? That Jewish boys belonged to Jewish girls? That it wasn't fair to snub the girls and flirt with the boys? And who would she list as a stag?

It was Alice's turn at the blackboard. Under "Dates" she wrote "Andy Unger," and "Michael Unger" under "Stags."

"Aren't they your cousins?" Emily asked when Alice returned to her desk.

"So what? Cousins and brothers are especially good for the stag line. Of course babies are not eligible," she said pointedly. All Emily had was Evan.

"The deal is they have to dance with me at least once," Alice continued. "The rest of the time they can cut in on other girls. And maybe somebody else's cousin or brother will cut in on me." She frowned. "Fat chance, with girls like Margery and Cressida around!"

Finally it was Emily's turn at the board. She chalked in "David Hirsch" under Edson Boatwright, Jr., Margery's date. Of course, next to his name, she had to write "Great Woods." She left out "High School," though. That way it sounded more like a prep school. But who was she fooling? Cressida and the other League girls knew she had gone to public school.

If only she didn't need a stag! But everyone else had listed at least one. How about Ted Margolin, the *real* one? She knew he couldn't come, of course, but she could still invite him. She wrote in his name with a shaky hand.

"But he's my stag!" Gail cried out. "I haven't asked him yet but I will the next time I see him at Flora Freund's."

There was no point in arguing. Maybe Gail didn't know that Ted wouldn't be coming anyway. Emily dragged the eraser over his name. She would have to think of a boy from Great Woods, someone she had no intention of actually inviting. Like Stanley Schachter, Davy's best friend, who chewed erasers off pencils and picked the whiteheads on his forehead until they oozed.

Or what if she used a made-up name? A name with a "Jr." or a number after it? A name that didn't sound Jewish.

In bold strokes she wrote "Oliver Holmes IV" followed by "Stonington Academy," the name of a real boys' school on Long Island.

"No fair!" Cressida said. "You have to invite another boy, someone from your own background. Eugenia's absent today but I'm pretty sure she's planning to invite Ollie Holmes."

Clearly, Cressida was lying. But what could Emily do? She couldn't admit that "Ollie," as she now thought of her made-up stag, didn't exist.

"Never mind, you can have him," Cressida said with contempt. "I hear he's a real drip."

Wait till she sees Davy, Emily thought.

"On to the theme," Cressida said. She gave her dip a forceful whirl. "Since we're studying the Middle Ages, I think it should be *The Court Jester*. We can decorate the assembly hall with our coats-of-arms sketches."

As part of a unit on heraldry, the class had been designing family crests. Cressida's and Margery's and some of the other girls' families already had their own, but Miss Lockwood said they would have to create up-to-date ones that reflected more personal interests.

So far, Emily had sketched a pacifier in one segment and a cigar in the other. She planned to use a quotation from Sergeant Friday for the third.

"Can't we have a Caribbean theme instead?" Holly asked.

"Yes! Paper moons and palm trees and coconuts, and maybe hula skirts just like in Hawaii!" Margery said.

"Or a Greek Island!" said Eugenia. "We could do circle dances, like at Greek debutante parties."

"Greek girls don't have real debutante parties and you know it," Cressida said. "They come out at that International Ball."

"Well, that's better than not coming out at all," Margery said. "Like some girls we know."

"Touché," Cressida said.

"Why do we have to connect the theme to our studies?" Gail asked. "It's a dance, not a class."

"We always tie in dance themes with our studies," said Cressida.

"But last year, in eighth grade, when we were reading *Beowulf,* we voted against having a *Beowulf* theme because we thought it would be too warlike," Barbara said.

"Yeah, we were afraid the boys would get wild and reenact the Danes attacking Grendel," Alice said.

"So instead we had that dumb Central Park theme and the boys went wild anyway. Remember how they poured punch into the daffodil vases?" Cressida said.

"And peed in the ficus tree!" Lindsley said.

The class burst into hoots and snickers.

Cressida rapped on Miss Lockwood's desk with her hockey puck. "Order in the classroom!"

The laughter stopped instantly.

"But if we're doing a movie theme, why not *Rebel Without a Cause*?" Alice suggested. "We could paste the Bromley seal in the middle of the dance floor like that seal in the entrance to the public high school James Dean goes to and if you step on it you're disqualified from the raffle."

The Bromley seal, stitched on the pocket of the charcoal gray school blazer, featured a quotation from Shakespeare: "Study is like the heaven's glorious sun." Above it, a pudgy bumblebee buzzed over an open volume illuminated by rays of sunshine.

"Some raffle! The grand prize is a gift certificate to the Bromley-Chatham Exchange," Barbara said.

"And you would never go to the Exchange, would you?" Cressida asked.

"What's that supposed to mean?" Barbara asked.

"Because you only buy brand-new clothes. Nothing second-hand for girls like you!"

"That's not true," Barbara said indignantly. "I wear some of my sister's old clothes."

The window, which had been cracked open, let in frosty breezes, but it was Cressida's words that made Emily shiver. She tried to catch Alice's attention, but Alice was busy pushing a pencil through a former student's initials carved into the desk.

"What we wear to the dance should be dressy but not garish," Cressida went on. She still had a tan from skiing and her hair seemed blonder than ever. It wasn't fair for a girl like her to look so much like Carol Lynley, Emily thought.

"If we have that *Court Jester* theme, won't we have to dress up in clothes from the Middle Ages—pointy hats and gowns with things that flatten your bosom?" Holly asked.

Cressida shook her head. "We'll wear the same kind of dresses we wore last year, only this year I'm going to wear a sheath." She turned around and fixed Emily with her icy blue gaze. "What about you?"

"Me?" Emily wasn't sure what she would wear. Thanks to Evan's arrival, the trip to Fashions for Girls had been put off indefinitely.

"Because no poodle skirts are allowed," Cressida said, keeping her eyes on Emily. "So I'm sorry if that's what you were planning to wear."

"It wasn't," Emily said.

Phoebe looked up from where she had been gazing at the East River. "We didn't have that rule last year. Since when do the girls have a dress code? Just the boys—ties and jackets, et cetera," she said.

"Wearing a uniform to school every day is bad enough," Lindsley said.

"I wasn't thinking of uniforms. Just no poodle skirts. Homeroom is almost over. I think we've pretty much agreed on a *Court Jester* theme, using our coats of arms as decoration. Has everyone finished theirs? A show of hands, please."

Hands shot up but Emily kept hers in her lap.

"You haven't finished yours yet? They're due by the end of the week, you know."

"I still haven't decided about what to put in one of the sections," Emily mumbled.

"Put in your poodle skirt!" Cressida said.

"Perfect!" Margery said.

Others hummed approval. Emily refused to wait around for more. She bolted out of the classroom, smack into Miss Lockwood.

"Emily, did I hear that your class dance is to have a medieval theme? That's what I admire about Bromley girls—the way you apply your studies to extracurricular life, as it were. A pedagogue's dream!"

Forcing back tears, Emily returned to her desk.

11 ❀ A Jester's Cap

"Yes, our theme will be *The Court Jester*," Cressida said coolly. "That's medieval, all right."

"I assume you're referring to the popular new movie, and not to the member of the royal entourage whose head was the first to roll if the king hadn't been sufficiently entertained," Miss Lockwood said.

Long opal earrings bobbed against her purple turtleneck. Her hair was cut into a ragged pixie and she wore black tights instead of stockings. Katie, as her students called her outside of school, was bohemian and progressive—a true nonconformist, they said. But ever since the day she and Phoebe had bumped into her in the Armor Room at the museum, Emily knew that her heart was in the Middle Ages.

"By a fortuitous coincidence, today's discussion topic fits in perfectly with your class dance plans," Miss Lockwood said. She entered the words "pedagogue" and "fortuitous" under "Nifty New Words."

She smiled sheepishly. "In response to your repeated requests, as it were, I am devoting this class to the customs of chivalry and courtly love."

Titters erupted. Emily looked across the room at Phoebe. Not so long ago, they would have traded glances and giggles.

"Under the code of chivalry, a married lady of noble birth had a young knight to do her bidding, as it were. The knight jousted and waged war in his lady's name, but he courted her by mastering literary and musical skills, not just the art of warfare. In medieval couples, it may surprise you to hear, the knight was always the younger of the pair."

"My mother is two months older than my father!" Margery blurted out.

"You mean married women had boyfriends?" Lindsley asked.

"Courtly love equals adultery, as it were," Alice scribbled on a scrap of graph paper and passed it to Emily.

Miss Lockwood pushed her bangs aside. "This is not part of the regular lesson plan, as it were," she said with a pained look. "Your parents might not approve."

"We won't breathe a word!" Lindsley said.

"We swear on a stack of Bibles," said Margery.

Everyone nodded vigorously.

"Anyway, I see our main attraction has arrived," Miss Lockwood said, sounding relieved. "Bromley girls, we have a special treat today: a genuine modern-day troubadour!" Crimson splotches crept across her cheeks.

Emily spotted the outline of a man's head through the frosted pane at the top of the classroom door. It was Mr. Carslake.

"I bet you didn't know that the head of our music department is also the founder of the Medieval Music Ensemble of Manhattan," Miss Lockwood said.

"Good day, girls," Mr. Carslake said with a deep bow. The sight of him, with a jester's cap pulled over his balding scalp and his knock-kneed legs encased in royal blue tights, amused Emily.

"You know me only as a piano player, but I am, as they say, a jack-of-all-trades. Allow me to introduce my mandolin." He caressed the instrument as if it were a ventriloquist's dummy. "Say hello to these charming young maidens!" He spoke into the hollow section and dragging his bow across the strings, producing a screech.

"The medieval counterparts of folk singers wandered from village to village and accompanied their songs with this and other stringed instruments such as the lute," Mr. Carslake continued, impervious to the stifled laughter around him.

"Often they would sing a type of song called an *aubade*. The one we have chosen is about the morning parting of two———"

"But Al—Mr. Carslake," Miss Lockwood interrupted. "I can't help thinking that 'Lord Randal' would be a more appropriate example of the troubadour repertoire, as it were." Her hazel eyes flashed behind her glasses. "And as it happens, I have already mimeographed it."

"But such a gory song for our cosseted young ladies . . ." Mr. Carslake said.

"Cosseted, I should say not! Bromley girls are unflinchable! They have gumption to spare!" Miss Lockwood said. She ran over to the blackboard and added "unflinchable" and "cosseted" to "Nifty New Words." "Cressida, would you be good enough to distribute these sheets?"

"That oh-bad must be a love song," Alice whispered. "See how Al is staring at Katie? That's why she doesn't want him to sing it."

"I will defer to your better judgment," Mr. Carslake said, with another sweeping bow.

He picked up one of the mimeographed sheets, plucked at his mandolin, and sang,

> O where have you been, Lord Randal, my son?
> O where have you been, my bonny young man?

He paused. Miss Lockwood's eyes stayed fixed on Mr. Carslake's flushed face as she discussed the song's deft use of rhythmic repetition—which, she warned, would lead to a bloodcurdling ending.

Mr. Carslake strummed and sang on:

> What will you leave your true love, Lord Randal, my son?
> What will you leave your true love, my bonny young man?
>> The tow and the halter to hang on yon tree,
>> And let her hang there for the poisoning of me.

"In a manner of speaking, Lord Randal flees his beloved

and seeks comfort with his mother," Miss Lockwood said. "But it's at his mother's house that he meets his death. Note that an S is all that separates 'smother' from 'mother.'"

"An astute, if unconventional, observation, Ka—Miss Lockwood!" Mr. Carslake said.

"Well, girls, what would you say to medieval music at the class dance? Shall we persuade Maestro Carslake to play a pavane or a rondeau?"

"How about "'Here Comes the Bride'?" Emily hummed softly.

"Miss Lockwood, ever since our first dance in sixth grade, we've had Chester Chanin's band," Cressida said. "They play fox trots and lindy hops. Polkas and waltzes, too. But never dances from the Middle Ages."

Davy Hirsch dancing a pavane or even a polka? There was something drastically wrong with that picture.

"But maybe we should take a vote," Cressida continued. She turned to Emily. "Do you like Chester Chanin?"

"Sure," Emily said. She had no idea if she liked him or not. She had never heard of him before now.

"How would you know?" Cressida asked.

"Everybody knows," Emily managed to say.

"I bet you haven't even——"

"Cressida, that's enough!" Miss Lockwood said. "There's no need to put our new girl on the spot. Back to Lord Randal, as it were. What's your hunch, Bromley girls? Was he poisoned or not?"

"It's ambiguous," Phoebe said.

What's not ambiguous is that you're starving yourself, Emily felt like saying. Maybe that's not so different from poisoning, she thought.

12 ❀ Connective Tissue

"Just because you're such a skinny malink doesn't mean I can see through you!" said a burly man in stained denim overalls standing behind Phoebe in front of a window display of pies.

Emily had been on her way to the stationery store to buy more colored pencils and tracing paper for her coat of arms when she spotted Phoebe ahead of her, standing in front of the Horn and Hardart Automat.

She looked like a Mongol pencil with her head as the eraser. Her camel hair coat hung as if her body had trouble supporting it. She had spent most of the vacation with her father and he probably didn't know how to cook. But deep down, Emily knew she was so thin because of her diet.

With its vast selection of cakes and pies, the Automat was hardly a place for dieters. It was a place for lonely people who didn't mind sharing tables with strangers or were too poor to afford regular restaurants or coffee shops, or for mothers with small children who wanted to show them how the miniature windows with the coin slots worked.

Phoebe quickly stepped aside to give the man an unobstructed view of the window. She seemed pleased rather than offended by his comment. Of course! He had called her skinny. She couldn't have wished for a bigger compliment.

Emily watched Phoebe follow the man through the revolving door. Keeping a safe distance, she followed close behind. She had learned a thing or two from Sergeant Friday. Would

Phoebe actually eat something here? Would she try the macaroni and cheese, whose tempting aroma wafted from a steam
table?

A wrinkled woman with sparse white hair—you could see
through to her rosy scalp—slumped at a table, staring into a
coffee mug. At the wall of condiments, the man in the overalls
cranked a brass handle, trying to coax globs of ketchup into
a glass of water. He stirred the mixture with a spoon until it
looked like tomato soup.

A girl Emily's age plunked nickels down a slot on the wall.
Twisting the chrome handle on one of the tiny windows, she
pulled out a plate of huckleberry pie. Almost immediately, another plate appeared. She pressed a spigot shaped like a lion's
head and filled a glass with chocolate milk.

Compared to Phoebe, the girl looked chubby. Actually, she
was just average. But average wasn't thin enough for Phoebe.
She probably thought Emily was fat these days.

Phoebe followed the girl to the wall of desserts. Plates of
rice pudding speckled with cinnamon, strawberry shortcake,
lemon meringue pie, foamy Boston cream pie, and apple pie
à la mode peeked out from behind individual windows. Was
Phoebe going to keep on gaping?

There were girls in their class, like Gail, who complained
about having "wobbly" thighs and lived on salads for days.
Then she'd gobble down two Mars bars in a row.

Not Phoebe. But hadn't she reached her goal yet? She
looked thinner than her cousin had ever been. Did she want
to be the thinnest girl in the history of Bromley? How could
she resist all those pies? Emily thought of the gnawing pit
in her stomach when she was hungry. She felt such a twinge
right now. If she hadn't been afraid Phoebe would see her, she
would have treated herself to a slice of Boston cream pie. But
if Phoebe could live with hunger pangs, so could she. Hunger
was like any other unpleasant sensation—like an itch from
a mosquito bite or a dull headache, and who couldn't put up
with those? Behind those little windows, the doughnuts and

pies were replaced in split seconds. Was that the way pounds
of fat came and went? Did they evaporate into thin air? Thin
as air: Was that what Phoebe was trying to be?

Emily spied the doughy hand of a woman in a white uniform, slipping plates with slices of cakes behind the windows.
There was no magic to it. There was a person, and a fat one,
at that, who replaced the cakes and pies and probably gorged
on them herself.

Emily was so busy watching the woman she missed the
moment when Phoebe must have pushed through the revolving doors and left. Did she have time to wolf down a piece of
pie? Would Sergeant Friday take the chance of losing someone he was chasing? Emily dashed out into the street.

Phoebe had only made it halfway up the block. She turned
around as if to check for pursuers. Emily ducked into an al-
leyway. Phoebe stopped in front of the Madison Avenue bak-
ery where Emily's mother had bought her birthday cake. She
ogled the éclairs and cream puffs in the window.

Careful to keep a safe distance, Emily followed Phoebe
past Fashions for Girls, where she barely glanced at the party dresses in the window, past the shoe store where Emily
had bought navy blue Keds in the fall, past the rental library
where Lady Lenore borrowed books in plastic covers for a
nickel a day.

She followed Phoebe past Schrafft's, and watched her press
her nose to the window of the candy store that carried jelly
candies in all flavors, even sarsaparilla. Then Phoebe glanced
in the butcher shop, where raw sides of beef and pork swayed
from hooks, and at the sacks of potatoes and onions outside
Novick's, the grocery store.

Mr. Novick, the owner, supposedly set aside only the best
fruit and vegetables for Lady Lenore. She had a saying: "Flirt
with the grocer, fight with the butcher." But she never shopped
in person. Every morning, perched on the same step stool in
the pantry from which Emily had called Ted, she ordered food
over the phone.

"Irv, I bet you have better peaches than those rotting ones you sent me!" she'd say. But she threatened the butcher: "If I catch you sending me tough brisket like that again . . ."

Emily's mother believed in being brutally frank, even with close friends. She told Aunt Irene she shouldn't wear slacks because her hips were too wide. She also told her that Emily was too old for Nancy Drew. That bluntness usually embarrassed Emily, but it had its good points. Her mother wasn't a phony. You knew where you stood. What would happen if Emily spoke exactly what was on her mind? What if she didn't worry about hurting people's feelings or didn't care what they thought of her? What if she was always outspoken and frank?

If you didn't say what you thought, weren't you being false? If so, Emily was false every day of her life. "I like your haircut!" she said, when she thought Alice should not have cut her stick-straight hair quite so short. "Sure," she said when Barbara asked to borrow a dime for a pack of M&M's, when what she wanted to say was, "You still haven't paid me back for last time."

What if she told Phoebe point blank she knew why they weren't friends anymore? But Phoebe was way ahead now, about to pass Sal's Pizza Pie Parlor. What torture that must be for her, Emily thought. Phoebe had been such a pizza fiend. She could avoid all those food places by walking up Park Avenue, which only had apartment buildings. But maybe she didn't want to avoid them. Maybe all she was thinking about was food.

The morning, weakly warmed by the puny winter sun, reminded Emily of the day before vacation, when Phoebe had brushed away her phony smoke rings, as if to brush away their friendship. But wasn't it more fun to laugh at the James Dean mourners than to window-shop for food?

Running as fast as she could until there was no distance between them, Emily grabbed Phoebe by the arm. Even through her coat, Emily could feel the stringy, fragile stuff between the bones. What if Emily told Phoebe she was wasting away?

What if she told her the truth? "You're way too thin! You look like a skeleton!" she could say.

The words froze in her mouth, as Phoebe pulled up her coat collar and ran as fast as her spindly legs, with her kneesocks puddled around the ankles, would allow. Emily watched her as she joined the crush of teenagers in polo coats and striped scarves clogging the main entrance to St. John's Episcopal Church. She watched her greet the other League members. They were probably there for a Young People's Auxiliary meeting.

It's no use. I'm a hopeless coward, Emily told herself.

Connective tissue. Now she remembered. That's what the stringy, fragile stuff between the muscles was called. She had learned about it in biology.

13 ❃ Alias James Dean

"Long time no see!" Davy said. He shoved an ivory corsage wrapped in cellophane in Emily's face.

The doorman had buzzed to announce Davy's arrival. Emily squinted through the peephole as he approached the front door. Was she seeing things, or was that a bright red motorcycle jacket he was wearing? With a two-tone sports jacket in tan and brown under it and a bowtie with a pattern of sports cars?

His sandy hair was slicked into a ducktail with sideburns stretching past his ear lobes. Whatever had possessed him? Was he trying to look like James Dean, or maybe that new singer Elvis Presley? It wasn't working. He looked better as a bookworm and a drip. There was no way Emily could have predicted a getup like that. Everyone else's dates would be wearing navy blue blazers and striped ties. He would be the only boy dressed like a hood or a juvenile delinquent.

"Hello, Davy!" Lady Lenore swished in wearing one of the satiny, loose-fitting floor-length dresses she called hostess gowns. She eyed Davy's outfit. Her mouth fell open, then closed abruptly, like a puppet's.

"An orchid! How lovely!" she said. "Here, let me pin it on." She stuck the pin dangerously close to where Emily had padded her bra with Kleenex.

"Your folks drive you in?" Lord Sidney said. His cigar bobbed at the corner of his mouth.

"Yes, they're double-parked right in front of the building," Davy said. "After they take us to the dance, they're going to see *The Diary of Anne Frank*. They'll pick us up at the stroke of eleven."

"Pick us up?" Emily felt woozy. No one got dropped off or picked up by their parents. Of course, no one's date's parents lived in the suburbs, either. Everyone else would be taking taxicabs to the dance. People in the city didn't drive their cars everywhere. Even Emily's parents left their Packard in a nearby garage for weeks at a time. And Davy's parents were embarrassing. His mother tinted her gray hair a bluish purple and asked too many questions. His father belched a lot.

"That's wonderful!" Emily's mother was saying. "I worry about you kids taking cabs at night! Please send your folks my very best."

Davy couldn't go to the dance dressed like that! Maybe he could borrow one of Lord Sidney's jackets. Of course, Emily's father was bigger than Davy.

"Say 'Bromley'!" Lord Sidney instructed, pushing Emily and Davy together and pointing his new camera at them, the one that developed photographs in less than a minute. There were piles of those instant Polaroid shots already—mainly of Evan. The Blob sleeping. The Blob crying. The Blob sucking on his bottle. The Blob stark naked.

Lord Sidney carefully peeled off the picture's moist backing. What started as a blur turned into Emily and Davy, propped next to each other like mannequins in a department store window. A stripe of black fuzz ran above Davy's lips like bathtub grime and Emily's hair still had clumps of frizz even though she had spent the entire afternoon in hair clips.

Why had she insisted on getting a straight dress? She looked straight all right—straight as a ruler. When they had finally made it to Fashions for Girls, her mother had begged her to try on a full skirt, but Emily refused.

"Hey, that's impressive!" Davy said, examining the picture.

"Physical chemistry, pure and simple," Lord Sidney said.

"I'm sure you have an elementary comprehension of the basics of photography."

Davy nodded emphatically. His Adam's apple jutted over his bowtie.

Lord Sidney continued: "When the positive and the negative are pulled through rollers, a capsule of chemicals erupts and spreads across the positive print sheet. Of course, for black and white prints, you need a different kind of silver grain."

"That goes without saying," Davy said.

Fräulein walked by with the Blob draped over her shoulder. "The famous Evan Joel Winter, I presume?" Davy said, offering his hand. Did he really think Evan would shake it?

"*Ja,* and you are the famous Davy, who Emily says is such a genius," Fräulein said. "You were once on a quiz show, she tells me!"

If looks could kill, Fräulein would have been drawing her last breath on the foyer floor. What Emily had told her was that Davy thought he was a genius.

"The very same," Davy said. "I don't believe in false modesty." He took a deep bow. It sent his eyeglasses crashing. When he picked them up, a crack ran diagonally across one lens.

"Oh, dear," Emily's mother said. "How will you manage?"

"Emily's not wearing her glasses, is she? Our prescriptions are about the same. Remember how we got our specs the same year and tried each other's on? Maybe I can use hers."

Emily hadn't forgotten that awful day, all right. Back in fifth grade, wearing her first pair to school. They were pearly pink. One boy called her Four Eyes.

"You're going to wear my plaid frames?" Over my dead body, Emily thought.

"Buddy Holly and another one of those Rock and Roll guys has plaid frames. What's good enough for them is good enough for me. Let me try them on."

No, this wasn't happening! Davy Hirsch wasn't here in Emily's living room in a James Dean costume asking if he could wear her glasses. She was beginning to feel achy. Maybe she was coming down with something. In that case, she should stay home. But Davy's parents would be at the theater, so he'd have to stay with her.

Davy picked up Emily's glasses from where she had left them on the chest in the foyer. "Hey, what do you think?" he asked. He pushed them over the bump on his nose. They looked even worse than his own flesh-colored frames.

"They go with your outfit!" Emily's father said. "Don't they, Twizzle?"

"They do not!" Emily said. And her father had promised not to call her Twizzle in front of other people. She stared down at her satin pumps, which had been dyed the same shade of blue as her dress.

"Anyway, they're too tight around the temples," Davy said with a sigh. "Might give me a headache. I'll just wear my broken glasses."

"No one will notice," Lady Lenore said. "Emily won't be the only nearsighted girl bumbling around the dance floor."

"For your information, the others might have to bumble without me!" Picking up her glasses, Emily ran into her room. She flung herself on the bed, burying her face in Scottie. She should have known better than to invite Davy.

Staying home was out of the question, though. Cressida and the League members might not notice if she was there, but they would certainly notice if she wasn't. That's the way it worked—people paid attention to what was weird and unusual. What was ordinary or typical they ignored. Besides, Rob would be there as one of the stags.

Lady Lenore came in. For a split second, Emily thought she might pat her on the back, but she sat at the edge of the bed, as if to leave any second. "Pull yourself together!" She said. "Davy does look ridiculous, I admit. I'm surprised his parents would let him out of the house like that. But I have news for you—you won't be the center of attention. People aren't examining you all the time, noticing every little thing.

Besides, *you* look fine, although I wish you had listened to me and gotten a dress with a full skirt."

Was it too much to expect a little sympathy? Snatching a balled-up tissue from her night table, Emily blew her nose and wiped her eyes. It was just as well her mother didn't let her wear mascara. It would be streaming down her cheeks. She tightened her garters and straightened the seams of her stockings.

She put on her glasses to get a better look at herself. She looked sickly, washed out, she thought. She applied another coat of Tangee colorless lipstick. Not that it did any good. In the tube, Tangee was the color of orange wax bottle candy, but, by some mysterious process probably invented by mothers, it turned clear as soon as you put it on.

Maybe by some magical feat of the imagination she could pretend she was Cressida. She could pretend Cressida's perfect features were her own. She could pretend her hair was Cressida's sleek pageboy, her eyes a cool blue without a misplaced brown freckle. For that matter, she could make believe she was Carol Lynley, with a perfect 34-22-34 figure and blond bangs sweeping across her forehead and a frizz-free corkscrew ponytail.

If only Lady Lenore would let her wear real lipstick! At this very moment, Melissa was probably applying Goubaud's Go-Go-Go Pink, getting ready for a date with Mark Whatshisname.

Emily pulled the Kleenex out of her bra. It had looked suspiciously lumpy. She plumped up her corsage. Suppose she was the only girl with a corsage?

She removed her glasses and hid them in her night table drawer next to the marble heart fragments. There was no way she would let Davy wear them. She had almost summoned up the courage to walk back into the living room when she heard Fräulein screech. "Uh-oh, I wouldn't bounce him up and down like that! He just had his last feeding!"

"I'll be careful," Davy said.

"That's too high, I warn you! He might whoops!"

It wouldn't be so terrible if Evan upchucked on Davy, Emily thought. Then he wouldn't be able to wear his jacket. He'd look less ridiculous in just a shirt and tie. Maybe there'd be puke on his bowtie too, and he'd have to borrow one of Lord Sidney's neckties.

But when Emily returned to the foyer, Evan and Fräulein were nowhere to be seen, and Davy was still in his motorcycle jacket and bowtie, trying on a perfectly normal pair of horn-rimmed glasses.

"Fräulein here had an extra pair," he explained. They were boy's glasses, Emily was quite sure. Had they belonged to a dead brother? She wondered. "The prescription's a little stronger than what I'm used to, but, who cares, I can see!"

And they looked way better than his broken glasses, Emily thought.

"Hey, Mr. Winter, you should think about inventing a plastic prescription lens that can't break," Davy said on his way to the front door.

"When I do, I won't forget to give you some of the credit, Davy!" Lord Sidney stroked his chin. "Meanwhile, you kids have a ball at the dance, I mean at the ball. How clever can I be—'a ball at the ball'?"

Emily didn't have to cringe with embarrassment about her father in front of Davy. Davy's father was even more embarrassing. She pressed the elevator button. Was her mind playing tricks, or did she detect a faint whiff of spit-up?

14 ❀ Family Crests

"Looks like I should have worn my suit of armor," Davy said, eyeing the *Court Jester* posters and coats of arms taped to the walls.

Armor would have been better than what he had on, Emily thought as Chester Chanin led the band in "Anything Goes." Couples crowded the dance floor.

Cressida danced by with Player Crosby. "That drippy date of Emily's is trying to look like James Dean," Emily heard her say. "And she's no Natalie Wood."

"Oh, I don't know. She's not half-bad looking," Player said.

Was Emily hearing things, or did the one and only Player Crosby actually pay her a kind of compliment? She began to feel better.

"Don't you even think about cutting in on her!" Cressida said. She made no effort to keep her voice down. "She's one of *them.*"

Phoebe, steered stiffly by her date Nick Crawford, drifted by, thin as a thread. A beige chiffon dress, probably Cousin Millie's, floated around her.

"Phoebe lost tons of weight!" Margery said.

"She looks like a model," Eugenia said enviously.

"She does not!" Alice objected, as her cousin Michael's hand lightly touched her waist. "Even Carol Lynley is fatter than that!"

"She's a bag of bones—nothing up there!" said Margery's date. He leered at Margery's D-cup breasts. She had the biggest bust in the grade.

107

Circling the dance floor, the stags paced like tigers at the Central Park Zoo. A boy with a pronounced cowlick broke away from the group to cut in on Cressida. Player Crosby sulked as he retreated to the stag line.

Mr. and Mrs. Gleason and Mrs. Barrett, the parent chaperones, ladled punch from a bowl surrounded by Christmas sconces and toy knights from Holly's younger brother's collection.

"Philomene Barrett" read a tag pinned next to a cameo brooch on Phoebe's mother's velvet-draped bodice. Holly's parents wore identification tags, too. They stood next to Miss Lockwood, the faculty chaperone. Silver-white earrings shaped like snowballs swung against her long neck as she thumped her toes in high-heeled pumps, which Emily had never seen her wear before.

Davy took Emily aside. They still hadn't danced. "Looky, looky!" he said. Pulling a slim silver container that looked like a perfume bottle from his jacket pocket, he uncapped it and sprinkled its contents over the punch.

"What do you think you're doing?" Do you want to get me expelled?" Emily said.

"I thought dates always brought flasks to these private school dances!"

Holly's father extended a large, veiny hand. "I'm afraid I must confiscate that piece of contraband, James Dean."

Davy's hand shook slightly as he handed him the flask.

Mr. Gleason drained it and handed it back. "Now that it's empty, no rules are being broken, eh?" He said with a wink. "Our little secret."

"Scout's honor," Davy said, with a salute.

Miss Lockwood approached, her floor-length garnet velvet gown swishing. "Why don't you and Emily get up on the dance floor?"

"But what's with the music?" Davy said. "Does it have to be from the Middle Ages, too?"

Before Emily could stop him, he had climbed on the stage. "Hey, don't you know how to play 'Hound Dog' or 'Blue Suede

Shoes'?" he asked Chester Chanin. He demonstrated by swiv-
eling his pelvis.

"We do not perform rock and roll," the bandleader said.

"We do not perform rock and roll," Davy imitated under his
breath.

Miss Lockwood approached the stage. "I'm afraid only the
musicians are allowed up here," she said gently. "This next
number is jazzier. You can show off your terpsichorean skills."

With dread, Emily allowed Davy to maneuver her on to the
dance floor. Out of the corner of her eye, she spied a boy with
floppy black hair and a scar, who had broken away from the
stag line. He tapped Davy firmly on the shoulder. He smelled
of chewing gum. The butterflies in Emily's stomach were doing cartwheels. In less than a minute, his cheek, the one without the scar, would be brushing against Emily's. He would
hold her close and——

"Just what do you think you're doing?" Davy asked, glaring
at Rob Gruber.

"Cutting in, what do you think? But I'll cut out, if I must,"
Rob said. He raised his arms like a prisoner.

"He's a stag," Emily said, as Rob made his way to the back
of the assembly hall. "He's supposed to cut in."

"They sure have some weirdo customs here!"

"You're the weirdo!" Emily shot back. He had ruined her
only chance. Rob would never ask her to dance again.

"Line up, everybody!" Chester Chanin boomed into the
microphone. "Put your right foot forward / Put your left foot
out / Do the bunny hop / Hop, hop, hop / Let's all join in the fun
/ Father, mother, son . . ."

"Tommy-boy, here's one dance you're an expert at!" Mrs.
Gleason sneered at her husband. "All you have to do is grab
the girl in front of you!"

Mr. Gleason sneaked in behind Margery and placed his
hands below her bra instead of at her waist.

"Shame on you!" his wife snarled, yanking him out of the
line.

"Has anyone seen my daughter?" Phoebe's mother asked.

"She must be in the school somewhere," Mr. Gleason slurred.

"Her date Nick is a *man*—he's over sixteen!" Mrs. Barrett said.

"Maybe they're in the library," Miss Lockwood suggested.

"Wait till I get my hands on that SOB!" Mr. Gleason thundered.

"Why are you getting all worked up?" his wife said. "It's not Holly who's missing!"

Miss Lockwood beckoned to Chester Chanin. The Bunny Hop came to a dead halt.

"It seems that one of your classmates, a Miss Phoebe Barrett, has disappeared," the bandleader announced. "If any of you have any knowledge of this young lady's whereabouts, please inform us immediately."

"Maybe she vanished in thin air—she's so skinny!" Margery said.

"I saw her in the ladies' room," Eugenia said.

"I didn't see her or her date on the bunny hop line," said Lindsley.

Nick danced by with Gail. "Oh, there you are!" Mrs. Barrett said with some relief. "Where's Phoebe?"

"She said she was going to the ladies' room," Nick said. "She is taking an awfully long time."

"Goody gumdrops! This is turning out to be a real live mystery!" said Alice.

What a nincompoop, Emily thought. Didn't she realize that something terrible might have happened? Phoebe might have passed out in the bathroom, weak from hunger.

"We'll have to comb the school floor by floor," Miss Lockwood said. "All nine stories, if necessary."

"Don't you have a public address system?" Davy asked.

"Heavens, no!" Miss Lockwood. "We are not a bus station."

"Or an elevator?"

"Like a hotel? I should say not."

The stairwells were dimly lit, and no one knew where flashlights were stored. Miss Lockwood picked up a votive candle.

"Please get everyone to stay in the assembly hall," she told Cressida.

Holly's parents weaved slightly as they followed Miss Lockwood up the stairs.

"Yippee! No more chaperones!" rose a raucous cheer from the stag line.

"Hey, can I come, too?" Davy begged. He ran after the search party. "I happen to be an expert on the Sherlock Holmes method. Deductive reasoning—that's my specialty."

"Can I be of assistance?" Alice asked Davy coyly. "I'm a Sherlock Holmes fan!" Was she actually flirting with him? What if she was? Those two deserved each other, Emily thought. They started up the stairs, two steps at a time. Holly, Margery, and Lindsley followed close behind.

"What do you think you're doing, tagging behind the Clothes Girls? Do you want to get thrown out of the ACGL?" Cressida whispered.

By now almost everyone had joined the search party. Miss Lockwood raised her flickering candle as they picked their way through the shadows, past the lower school library and classrooms on the third floor, past the science labs on four, past Miss Foxworthy's office on five, past the bookstore on six.

They stopped outside Nurse Lambroza's office on the ninth floor. "There's no need to panic!" Davy said. "It is my considered opinion that the answer lies right under our noses. When you played hide-and-seek as a child, what was your favorite hiding place?"

"Not fit to tell the kiddos—heh, heh!" Mr. Gleason said tipsily.

"I bet Phoebe's smoking somewhere!" Mrs. Barrett said. "I caught her filching one of my cigarettes."

"Exhibit A!" Davy announced. Leading the procession toward the sound of rustling paper and the smell of a freshly lit match, he pushed open Nurse Lambroza's door.

Phoebe was sitting cross-legged on the floor, surrounded by black-and-white photographs. She had struck a match to one of them and a corner was curling up.

Her mother screamed. "Phoebe, what do you think you're doing? You could set the school on fire, lighting up next to inflammable objects!"

"I'm never sure if it's 'inflammable' or 'flammable,'" Miss Lockwood said.

"Thinking of Nifties at a time like this!" Alice muttered.

"But I'm not smoking!" Phoebe said. "I was trying to burn my posture picture."

Miss Lockwood gasped. She blew out the match and pried the picture from Phoebe's hand. She eyed the photos scattered on the floor. "They're supposed to be locked up!"

"They were in a plain old folder. I just wanted to find *my* picture," Phoebe said. "I swear, as soon as I found it, I didn't look anymore."

Did Phoebe think she looked fat in the picture? Emily wondered. A brief glimpse showed that she looked completely normal.

"Help, someone!" Miss Lockwood pleaded frantically. Boys were falling on top of one another, trying to scoop up the photographs.

"Let's find the twelfth graders!" Lindsley's date said.

"Find Margery's!" shouted a stag.

"Don't you dare!" Cressida said. "You're just a bunch of perverts!"

"Emily, maybe you should try to find yours!" Davy said. "Alice, you too!"

Michael, Alice's cousin, burst into the room, breathless, after running up the stairs. "Chester Chanin's having a fit, he's ready to distribute the sombreros," he said.

Miss Lockwood gathered the pictures into a neat pile and returned them to the folder. "I'll make sure they're kept under lock and key."

"I think Phoebe had the right idea," Lindsley said. "We should burn them."

"Phoebe, I'm afraid you're in for a little trouble, as it were," Miss Lockwood said. "I'm going to have to report this incident to Miss Foxworthy."

"I understand," Phoebe said sheepishly. She looked fragile
and weak, as if she could be ripped into smithereens as easily
as one of the pictures, Emily thought as she ran downstairs
with the others. On the assembly hall stage, Chester Chanin
clapped a pair of castanets together. "Time for the Mexican
Hat Dance! All you señors and señoritas, form a circle around
the sombrero!"

The "sombrero" was a tennis hat in Bromley gray and
white, with a pompom and Chester Chanin's name stitched
in italics. Couples and stags gathered around it. "Hey, this is
fun!" Davy said, kicking wildly. "Especially since I'm taking
Spanish next year." He switched partners with Alice, leaving
Emily to dance with Michael. Apparently he had gotten the
hang of cutting in.

Chester Chanin tossed out duplicates of the pom-pommed
tennis hat. "One per customer!"

"I have too many already," Cressida sniffed, flinging hers
in the air like a bridal bouquet.

Davy caught it. "I think I'll start a collection," he said.

"Cold enough for you out there?" Vince said as he pulled the
elevator lever and began the slow ride up to the fifteenth floor.

The ride home had seemed endless, too. Sure enough, Davy
had found his parents waiting in front of the school in their
powder blue Cadillac convertible. "You're early," Mrs. Hirsch
said. "In another five minutes, she would have said 'You're
late,'" said Mr. Hirsch. Davy's parents were always bickering.

"Hey, you wouldn't believe what happened!" Davy said.

"You can't make a left on York Avenue!" His mother yelled,
grabbing the wheel and jerking it to the right. "Wouldn't believe what?"

Emily jabbed Davy deep in the ribs. "Ouch! Someone was
caught smoking, that's all," he said.

In the vestibule outside the Winters' apartment, Emily
avoided the three-quarter-length mirror her mother had in-
stalled. Vince was waiting. It didn't pay for him to go down

again if no one else rang. Obviously, he could tell that Davy wouldn't take long.

"Hey, um, you don't mind if I call up your friend Alice, do you?" Davy asked. He looked hopelessly silly in his motorcycle jacket with a Chester Chanin sombrero plopped on his head.

"It's a free country," Emily said as he got in the elevator.

Her mother appeared in the foyer in her nightgown. "Did you have fun?" she asked with a cavernous yawn.

"I should never have invited Davy," Emily said.

"Well, you had no choice. Grandma Anna used to say: go with the sheep and meet the flock."

After those comforting words, Emily wasn't about to tell her mother about Rob. Anyway, what was there to tell?

"Well, nighty-night," her mother said. Emily could hear her father's stop-and-start snores competing with the whine of the signal pattern from the television in Evan's room. Fräulein had probably fallen asleep watching *The Late Show*. She'd be up soon; Evan still screamed for a bottle at midnight.

"I owe you, how you say, an apology," Fräulein said sleepily when Emily walked in. "All through *The Late Show*, I am thinking about this. I didn't mean to embarrass you in front of your boyfriend. Forgive me, *bitte*."

"Once and for all, he is not a boyfriend! He's just someone I know from Great Woods. Besides, he likes Alice."

"Ach, such bad taste he has?" Fräulein said.

"Oh, he has bad taste, all right," I said. "Didn't you see what he was wearing!"

"That's the style, isn't it? That actor who died, James Dean—he is dressed in those kind of clothes in that movie about a teenage criminal."

Emily giggled. Had Fräulein actually seen *Rebel Without a Cause*? Maybe she went to the movies on her day off. "Would you like to try bringing up Evan's bubble?" she asked Emily.

"Oh, all right, I'll try, but not if it takes forever." Emily patted Evan on his upper back the way she'd seen Fräulein do. He burped instantly.

"Well done!" Fräulein said, as Emily handed her the

near-empty bottle. Thick smears of formula coated the inside. "You'll see—at the next dance you'll have more luck!"

Emily didn't see the connection between a successful burp and a good time at a dance. In bed, she hugged Scottie under the covers. He was still damp from her earlier crying spell. "Lucky you, you don't have to worry about boys and dances and best friends," she whispered in his ear. Or about being left out because you're Jewish.

Emily was still angry with Davy. Not because of his outfit or the flask or the cracked glasses or even his interest in Alice. She was furious because he had stopped Rob from cutting in.

Things could have turned out so differently . . .

Rob taps Davy on the shoulder and cuts in. His cheek, the one without the scar, brushes against Emily's. His hand rests gently yet forcefully on the small of her back.

The band strikes up The Blue Danube *waltz.*

"I owe you an apology," Rob says. He's very graceful for a boy; the waltz is his favorite dance. "I'm sorry about that idiotic practical joke."

He tricked Emily, he explains, because sometimes, like so many other people, he feels the need to pretend he's somebody else.

Sometimes he wants to be like Ted, who's Mr. Popular and doesn't have a disfiguring scar.

I don't mind the scar, says Emily, as Rob presses his cheek to hers.

15 ❀ Popsicle Pajamas

"What's that all over your face?" Lady Lenore asked Emily at breakfast the next morning.

"What's what?" Emily pushed a spoon around her soft-boiled eggs. Something was wrong. She wasn't the least bit hungry.

"Don't you look in the mirror first thing? You're all broken out."

In the small bathroom off the kitchen where Harriet soaked her rags and mops, Emily inspected the clusters of tiny scarlet pimples scattered across her face.

"Could be an allergy," her mother said. "What have you been eating at school?"

Maybe it was the Mars bars she had pigged out on last week. She and Alice had been stopping for candy every day. Chocolate and nuts together were supposed to give you acne.

"Maybe you should see Dr. Lieberman." For a bad cold Lady Lenore didn't suggest a visit to the doctor, but an unsightly rash was an emergency.

"It's just old-fashioned pimples, if you ask me," Lord Sidney said. "What's that cream called—Clearasil?"

"No, you don't get an acne rash just like that," Emily's mother said. "Maybe it's chicken pox. Does it itch?"

"I already had chicken pox. In second grade. Remember when the school nurse called and you were away shopping in the city? Harriet was there, but since she couldn't drive, I had to wait until you got home."

"Of course, I remember."

Emily didn't believe her. Her mother hadn't shown up by the time the school bus was ready to leave, so Emily had to get on with the rest of the kids. Many of them caught chicken pox, too.

"The only childhood disease I have left is mumps," Emily said.

Fräulein walked in with Evan under her arm. She swirled a baby bottle under the hot water tap with her free hand and stared. "Young lady, if I am not mistaken, you have the German measles!"

Emily had forgotten about that one.

"Fräulein, if I may say so, you have no business making a diagnosis!" her mother said with disdain. "You're not even a registered nurse!"

"I happen to know something about this disease," Fräulein insisted. "There was an epidemic during the war. The scientific name is rubella—it has nothing to do with Germany."

Lady Lenore pressed a finger to her lips. She was always shushing Fräulein about the war. Of course, Emily discouraged any talk of the war, too. It wasn't that she wasn't interested in what had happened to Fräulein, but if she listened, she would have to feel sorry for Fräulein, and she liked it better the other way around, with Fräulein feeling sorry for her.

"The first mother I worked for in New York caught rubella while she was pregnant," Fräulein said. "The child was born with serious defects. It is good for Emily to get it before she has a baby."

"That will do, Fräulein! Instead of playing doctor, you should be training Evan to sleep through the night," Emily's mother said.

"It will happen naturally. When he's ready."

"And you can't leave before that. May I remind you that you agreed not to take on another case before he sleeps through?"

Lady Lenore sounded desperate. Obviously, she was scared to death of taking care of Evan by herself, Emily thought.

"I will stay as long as you and Emily need me," Fräulein said.

"You mean, as long as Evan and I need you."

An uncomfortable silence followed.

"Ach, *ja*. How you say? My tongue slipped."

"You mean you had a slip of the tongue," Lady Lenore corrected.

It better be a slip! Was Fräulein implying that Emily needed a baby nurse for herself? That's exactly what she was implying. She didn't need Fräulein to feed her and burp her—she needed her to talk to and watch *Dragnet* with.

On the matter of Evan sleeping through the night, Emily had her own little secret: about a week ago he had not awakened for a night feeding. Emily had peeked in, kept up by brain-numbing algebra equations. She found Fräulein and Evan both sound asleep. She thought of turning on the television to wake Evan up. If he slept through the night, Fräulein would leave. As far as she knew, there wasn't a peep out of Evan until the sun rose. But if Fräulein noticed that he'd slept through, she didn't breathe a word. Then the next night, to Emily's relief, Evan woke up screaming again. And the next and the one after that.

"Fräulein, what are you standing there for?" Lady Lenore said. She dialed Dr. Lieberman's office from the kitchen phone. "Take Evan away! There's no reason for a boy to get the German measles!"

"*Ja,* Mrs. Winter," Fräulein said with a sigh.

"Dr. Lieberman's new assistant, Dr. Halpern, will be coming. He hasn't seen a German measles rash before and when he takes over Dr. Lieberman's practice, it will be important for him to be able to identify one."

"What am I—some kind of guinea pig?" Emily said.

"You might like him better than Dr. Lieberman."

Her mother had a point. "Fräulein, make sure Emily stays in bed!" she said before leaving for her Friday morning standing appointment at the beauty parlor. That appointment was sacred. The only time it had been broken, as far as Emily remembered, was when her mother was in the hospital, recovering from Evan's birth.

Emily called Alice. "I'm not going to school. I have the German measles, or rubella, or whatever it's called."

"Great!"

"I don't see what's so great about it. I feel crummy. How would you like to have an itchy rash all over you?"

"That's just it, I want to catch it. Don't you know that girls are supposed to get rubella before they have babies? Can I come over after school?"

The doorbell rang as Emily was drifting off. It was just like Alice to wake her up.

"Quick! Put on something nice!" Fräulein said, rushing to her bedside. "A very handsome young man has come to call."

"That's only the doctor!" Emily doubted he was so good looking. How could you trust the opinion of a woman who thought Sergeant Friday was the biggest dreamboat in the world?

Fräulein led in a tall, lanky man in khakis and sneakers. "Hi there, my name is Dr. Nathan Halpern," he said. "But you can call me Dr. Nat."

Fräulein wasn't wrong, after all. His eyes were a soft velvety brown and he looked too young to be carrying one of those black doctor bags. Emily hoped he wouldn't offer her a lollipop.

"I hear you might have the German measles. If so, you're one lucky girl!" he said. More praise for being sick! And couldn't he at least use the scientific name? Even Nurse Lambroza had offered congratulations when Emily's mother called to say she'd be absent.

Fräulein poked her head in. "Herr Doctor, you would like maybe some hot cocoa?"

"No, thanks," he said, extracting a stethoscope from his black bag.

The doorbell rang again. "Ach, such commotion!" Fräulein said. She scurried back to the foyer.

"I'm going to have to ask you to unbutton your top," Dr.

Nat said softly. Emily hadn't thought of this! Why couldn't he study the rash on her face instead?

Her cheeks were burning as she unbuttoned her red flannel pajama top with the popsicle pattern. If only she'd worn a polo shirt you could just pull up and down quickly.

"Guess what?" Emily heard Alice's squeaky voice telling Fräulein, "I'm not just here to bring over Emily's books. I'm going to do my homework with her so that I can get the German measles, too. By the way, did it really start in Germany?"

Emily heard footsteps down the hall. Alice stood in the doorway transfixed as Dr. Nat held a magnifying lens to her chest.

"Miss Winter, you have a classic rubella rash, all right," he said, as he put the lens back in his black bag. "Straight out of a textbook. Fortunately, at your age, it's a mild disease with no aftereffects. In three days, you'll be good as new. If you were married and pregnant, it could cause problems."

Emily wondered if he was married and had a baby. He wasn't wearing a wedding band, but her father didn't wear one, either.

"That's why I want to catch it," Alice said. "It's incredibly contagious, so being near Emily should do the trick. But just to make extra sure it happens, I'll drink from the same glass she does or use her toothbrush, if she'll let me."

"Good idea," Dr. Nat said. "One or two days of feeling under the weather in exchange for lifetime immunity." He reached into his bag and winked. "You girls aren't too old for lollipops, are you?" He handed Emily a cherry and Alice a lime.

"Can we trade?" Alice asked after he left.

"Take them both," Emily said with disgust.

"How could you just let that hunk stare at your bazooms?" Alice said.

"He wasn't staring, he was performing a professional examination. And it was my chest, not my breasts. Besides, it's his job. Don't you get undressed when you go for a checkup?"

"My pediatrician's a woman—Dr. Priscilla Sturges. Just about everyone in the class goes to her because she went to Bromley. I used to go to a man, but that was when I was Evan's age, so it didn't matter."

Emily made a note to ask her mother about switching to Dr. Sturges. But then she would never get to see Dr. Nat again. She already had a crush on him.

"It's a mild case," he told Fräulein as she handed him his overcoat. "She can probably go back to school in a day or two."

"I guess letting a doctor see you with your clothes off is better than having a bunch of Kensington boys leer at your posture picture," Alice said.

Emily hadn't thought about posture pictures since the emergency assembly held the week after the class dance. Officially, it had been called the Posture Picture Assembly, but secretly Emily and Alice renamed it the Nude Assembly.

The speaker was Elspeth Garvey, a Bromley graduate whose scoliosis was cured after it was diagnosed from her posture picture. She'd had to wear a back brace for two years and now her spine was ramrod straight.

"I am so, so grateful for Bromley posture pictures," she said. "Otherwise I would never have found out about my curved spine and I'd probably be bent over like an old lady by now." She had more posture pictures taken at Radcliffe her freshman year, she said.

"Students' posture pictures are as off-limits as their IQ scores," Miss Foxworthy said sternly.

"But if they're so top secret, how come they could be found so easily?" Margery blurted out, staring at Phoebe.

Everybody started talking at once.

"Yeah, how come Phoebe found them?"

"Our dates were gawking at them!"

"Suppose some dirty magazine gets hold of them!"

"Won't they be burned?"

Could some of the Kensington boys have gotten a look at her posture picture? Emily wondered for the first time since the dance. Had Miss Lockwood really managed to hide the pictures in time?

"They will be destroyed," Miss Foxworthy said. "And as

you are well aware, the student responsible has been sharply reprimanded."

All heads turned toward Phoebe, who was looking thinner than ever. She had been suspended for three days.

"You can't destroy them!" She shouted. "They're evidence!"

"You owe me thanks for a good deed: visiting a sick friend," Alice said, squeezing the toothpaste tube. The bottom was neatly rolled up like the lid of a sardine can. That was Fräulein's handiwork. She couldn't stand waste.

"I thought I was doing you the favor!" Emily said. She wished, not for the first time, that it was Phoebe who had come over. They would have been figuring out ways to see Dr. Nat again—sniffles, sore throats, stomachaches. What if Phoebe caught the German measles? She would probably lose even more weight.

"I have news for you," Alice said. She looped her green-and-white-striped Dartmouth scarf around her neck. "Your rash is icky. I'm not so sure I want to look like that. Anyway, it's ridiculous to try to catch something on purpose. Most of the time, people catch things they don't want to."

Like your mother, Emily thought.

"I changed my mind," Alice said. "I'm leaving." She screwed the cap back on the toothpaste. "I hope it's not too late."

16 ❀ Body Types

Emily's rash cleared up and she was back at school on Monday. Minutes before gym, though, she felt a warm squishiness between her legs. Her period was a few days early. It was only her fourth time ever and she didn't have a sanitary napkin. She ran into a bathroom behind the art studio.

Almost nobody used that bathroom, but somebody was in there now. Cigarette smoke fogged the air. Emily traced it to a stall with a pair of orthopedic brown oxfords protruding from the bottom. The shoes and the cigarette could only belong to one person: Miss Heath, the Current Events teacher. She always grabbed a few puffs between classes.

Emily was not about to plunk a dime down the machine with Kotex feminine napkins embarrassingly spelled out in giant letters while a teacher lingered in a stall smoking. Finally, she heard the roar of a toilet flushing. Miss Heath emerged with a copy of the *New York Times* rolled under her arm. Had she actually been reading in there?

"Morning, Winter," she said, baring her rusty teeth.

"Hello," Emily mumbled. She waited to drop the dime in the machine until Miss Heath was out the door. A wrapped sanitary napkin tumbled down, but without a belt. How would the napkin stay in place? Emily heard the bathroom door open. Not another teacher, she hoped. The teachers should have their own bathrooms, she thought.

She wrapped the soiled Kotex in toilet paper and dropped it into a small metal house-shaped structure on the floor. She flattened the new napkin inside her panties and pulled open the slide-lock on the stall door.

Standing at the sink, holding a photograph with one corner scorched, was Phoebe. She didn't look at Emily. For a long time now, her diet seemed to have squeezed her into her own tight, narrow world, as if being aware of other people could put on pounds.

"Pheebs!" Emily leaned over her shoulder to look at the picture. She made out the vague outline of a half-naked girl. "I thought those photographs had been destroyed," she said.

"I managed to stuff mine in my purse," Phoebe said. "Miss Lockwood didn't notice."

The photo was captioned "Endomorph." Under that, it said, "Sturdy Nordic Aryan Body Ty——." The last two letters had been burned off.

"What's that supposed to mean?" Emily asked. What was an endomorph? It sounded like an insect, a rare kind of butterfly.

"Just some scientific description of my formerly fatso self," Phoebe said with a shrug. Her shoulders stuck up like the tips of a bent wire hanger.

It was useless to point out that she had never been fat. And certainly, now, she was far from sturdy. A strong breeze could probably knock her over.

Emily said, "How come there's no comment about your posture?" It was the first time she had really spoken to Phoebe since her birthday party. It didn't matter that they were in the bathroom. It didn't matter what they were talking about. She was happy just to be with Phoebe.

Phoebe slipped the picture in the middle of *Beginning Algebra*. "Time for gym," she said. She laced up her sneakers. Since when did Phoebe feel the need to rush to basketball? In the fall, she had signed excuse slips every two weeks and Nurse Lambroza had suggested she see a doctor if she was getting her period that often. Emily didn't believe for a minute that Phoebe actually liked gym, but it was exercise. Running around a basketball court burned up calories.

"Lucky me, I get to sign an excuse slip. I have the curse," Emily said. She didn't have cramps but she was only too glad to skip basketball. Not that she would get to miss it completely. She would have to stay in the gym, pretending to watch, or doing her homework.

"Oh, right, excuse slips!" Phoebe said, sounding wistful.

"How come you don't skip gym anymore when you have your period?" Emily asked.

"I don't get it anymore."

"What do you mean, you don't get it?"

"My period. It stopped."

"Stopped?"

"You heard me. I haven't been getting my period."

"Since when?" Emily knew Phoebe had started before she met her, in eighth grade.

"Since about two months ago. And I don't miss it a bit. Good riddance, I say!"

"I guess." But it wasn't normal. Once it started, your period was supposed to show up every month. A visit from Aunt Stinky, some girls called it.

Unless you were pregnant, of course. Then you stopped menstruating. But how could Phoebe be pregnant? She'd never even kissed a boy, she'd told Emily. Besides, she'd be showing by now. Lady Lenore had sprouted a belly right away.

Your period stopped for good when you went through something called change of life. You got cranky and sweated bullets even when it wasn't hot. Once, when Grandma Anna was snapping at everyone, Lady Lenore said, "That's what happens when you lose your period." But that didn't happen till you were fifty.

Emily studied their reflections in the mirror.

Two girls of the same age and height.

One dark, the other fair. Like Rose Red and Snow White.

One slender, the other emaciated.

Phoebe smiled at Emily—like in the old days, except that her cheeks were so gaunt, there were only faint indentations where her dimples should have been. For a split second, Emily half expected her to ask for the Laurence Olivier pinup or to suggest they go see *Rebel Without a Cause.*

Instead she was rummaging in her Bromley book bag. "I managed to save one more picture."

She fished it out. It was Emily in profile, half naked—her posture picture. She couldn't bring herself to look too closely. The outline of her small bust was enough. Her mother called them beginner breasts. And she was right about Emily's posture; she was slouching.

The caption read, "Ectomorph: Eastern European body type with Semitic slump."

"Can I keep it?" she asked, but Phoebe was already out the door.

Now Emily understood what Phoebe had meant by "the evidence" at the Posture Picture Assembly. She hadn't been referring to her previous plumpness; she meant the captions. Emily tucked the picture inside *Modern Biology.* She also helped herself to Miss Heath's copy of the *Times,* which had been left on the sink. She could read it during gym for her Current Events homework. This week's assignment was "What I Would Fight For." You had to pick a newspaper or magazine article illustrating a contemporary cause and write a short essay about it.

Emily tucked the paper under her arm. She would read it during gym.

17 ❀ Gymsuits

Emily browsed through the headlines. There had to be something that would fit the Current Events assignment. She was sitting at the opposite end of the bench from two League members who had also signed excuse slips. Margery was taking notes from *Life in the Middle Ages*. Eugenia pretended to be doing her math, but inside her textbook was the February *Photoplay*.

"Barrett, cover your zone!" Miss Stillman bellowed. "And get a move on! Three seconds in a lane is a violation! You know the rules!"

"Yes, Miss Stillman," Phoebe said.

Didn't she realize that Phoebe might be too weak to move faster? Didn't she notice that she was wasting away?

"In the center, string bean!" Miss Stillman ordered. So she *had* noticed. "You're a guard this time around, remember?"

"Actually, I was going to ask if I could be excused," Phoebe said.

"The curse again? Aren't you the one who's been signing all those slips?"

"I haven't signed any lately. It's just that I feel dizzy."

"All right, take a minute on the bench."

Why didn't Miss Stillman send Phoebe to Nurse Lambroza? Emily wondered. Clearly, she was well aware of how skinny she had gotten. Why didn't any of their teachers seem concerned? Phoebe got straight Veegees, that's why. Grades—

that's all Bromley cared about. If she were flunking out, it would be a different story.

The League members moved over to let Phoebe sit next to them at the other end of the bench. Emily saw her lower her head between her knees. From first aid training in Great Woods, she knew that was a trick to avoid fainting. Phoebe raised her head again. Her face was pale as a cloud.

Emily quickly decided against "The Integration Debate: An Analysis of Leading Candidates' Positions," about Senator Adlai Stevenson's views on ending segregation in the public schools in the South. She dismissed an article on whether President Eisenhower would run for a second term and another about Khrushchev's denunciation of Stalin's crimes at a communist party congress. Politics and more politics. Wasn't there anything about prejudice or discrimination? She was about to give up when she spotted an intriguing headline at the bottom of page 21.

"High School Honor Student Dies of Eating Disorder." She couldn't believe her eyes. She raced through the article. Her heart beat like a drum. She couldn't wait for Current Events. This was the perfect article for the "What I Would Fight For" assignment.

18 ❖ Galoshes

Long before the alarm clock pealed, Emily woke up to the scrape of snow shovels in the courtyard. Would Bromley be closed? In Great Woods, to keep school buses off icy roads, school closed at the drop of a flake. Normally, she would jump for joy at the prospect of a snow day, especially since she would be missing a biology test, but now she'd have to wait until next Friday for Current Events. They only had it once a week.

She dragged herself out of bed, yanked up the venetian blinds and rubbed away frost from the window. The flakes were so big, she could almost tell the ways in which they were different from one another as they fluttered past her window.

It was Fräulein's day off, and, in the kitchen, Emily's mother cradled Evan awkwardly in one arm, holding his bottle in the other. "Come on, you can drink a little faster than that." He let out a piercing wail. Emily waggled her fingers in her ears and made faces at him. He smiled his crooked, toothless smile. Next to Fräulein, Emily was his favorite.

"School might be closed," her father said over the top of the *Herald Tribune.*

Emily peered out the kitchen window. "I heard that as long as the city buses are running, Bromley stays open." As if on cue, two buses lumbered down Madison Avenue.

"School was never closed for me when I was growing up," her mother said.

131

"Who waited for official closings? We played hooky!"

"Go ahead, brag about that in front of your daughter! You're setting a fine example."

Emily thought of the truant officers in books. "Were you ever caught?"

"Nah, we just parked our schoolbags at the corner drugstore," her father said.

Emily tuned into WINS, the radio station that announced school closings. First came a string of public and parochial schools: "P.S. 41, P.S. 6, P.S. 199, St. Agnes. . . ." Then the private schools: Kensington, Chatham, Bromley!

"Emily, sweetheart, could you——"

"I'm going back to bed," Emily said firmly. She could tell her mother had some babysitting in mind. On Fräulein's day off, Emily had more than her share of Blob care. As soon as she came home from school, she fed him "high tea," as she called his four o'clock bottle. If Lady Lenore got a phone call in the middle of his bath, Emily took over, making sure he didn't drown. She patted his back while studying for midterms. She burped him with *Life in the Middle Ages* open on her lap. She wound and rewound his musical bunny mobile while memorizing Latin declensions. Lady Lenore was usually sound asleep and Emily still struggling over algebra problems when Evan woke up screaming, so she gave him his night bottle, too.

Real chores, Emily thought. Even harder than Phoebe's. But it was fun rubbing noses with Evan for Eskimo kisses. However, she could think of better things to do on a snow day.

The phone rang almost as soon as she crawled back under the sheets. It was Alice. "Why wait till tonight? Why not come over right now?" she asked. This was supposed to be the night of the first Flora Freund fake-out, and Emily was going to sleep over at the Ungers'. She didn't want to spend the whole day with Alice, but if she stayed home she'd be roped into taking care of Evan.

"Bring your sled!" Alice said.

"I gave mine away. I don't play with dolls anymore, either."

"Oh, come on! Spoken by the director of 'Avalon'! Everybody will be on Pilgrim Hill on a day like this! You can use Bettina's old sled."

Everybody? Did that mean Kensington boys? But Rob and Ted were certainly too old to go sledding—they were in tenth grade, Emily reminded herself.

She put on a pair of flannel pants, her winter parka, and pony-skin boots and sneaked out the door. Vince was busy clearing the driveway, packing snow drifts against the curb. Flakes frosted Emily's glasses as she trudged over to Alice's section.

She was taking advantage of Alice, Emily told herself. Borrowing books, using her as an alibi—it wasn't fair. On her side, the friendship was based on convenience. Or was she actually beginning to like her?

There were no crutches or wheelchair on the landing. Could Mrs. Unger have ventured out in this weather? Maybe she had an urgent doctor's appointment. Alice came to the door in her flannel nightgown. "Guess what? Louisa is letting us have fresh-baked brownies! She's staying over while Bettina and my parents are in Puerto Rico."

Was Louisa actually beckoning them into the kitchen? She placed a pair of piping hot brownies on a napkin and handed it to Emily without frowning. Instead, her expression was kind, concerned.

"How come you didn't go to Puerto Rico?" Emily asked.

"I didn't want to go. It's OK for Bettina to miss a day of school—she's a senior—she's almost through with her work for the year. Besides, I turn red as a lobster in the sun. Anyway, it's great being home almost by my lonesome. Louisa doesn't care what I do. And I love Central Park when it snows!"

Hogwash, Emily thought. Another example of how Alice's parents favored Bettina. Emily felt a sudden pang of yearning for Great Woods. On snow days, she'd coasted down the hill behind her house with Melissa and Davy. They'd warmed up in her kitchen with cocoa and toasted marshmallows.

Alice dragged in a wooden sled with metal runners. It was

too short for Emily. Either her head or her legs would hang over.

"This is for an eight-year-old!" she protested.

"We can trade off," Alice said. "Mine is longer."

They trailed the sleds through trees with spun-sugar branches. The park looked like a postcard from Vermont.

Children were dragging sleds, inner tubes, and large trays up Pilgrim Hill. "There's no one our age," Emily said. "Go sledding, if you must. I'm staying right here."

"Suit yourself. Here I go!" Lying on her stomach, Alice pushed off. She waved when she reached the bottom of the hill. It looked like fun, Emily had to admit. Who cared if she was too old for sledding? She stretched out on her sled, head first, with her calves folded up behind her. She gripped the steel rudder. By now, there was a traffic jam on the hill. All around her sleds whirled and collided, like bumper cars at an amusement park.

A sled with two boys jammed into Emily. Willy and Wally! They lobbed snowballs at her. "I'll tell Mademoiselle!" she threatened. Wet strands of hair clouded her glasses. She heard a dull thud. A sled had bumped into hers. Looking directly at her from his perch on the trashcan lid he was using was Rob Gruber. His eyebrows were half hidden under a ski cap, but the scar looked bigger than ever.

"Emily!" he said with a broad smile. "Did I hurt you?"

"N-no," Emily answered. He mumbled something. She thought she heard the word "together." Could he be suggesting they go down the hill together? But he took off immediately, following a fleet of trashcan lids down the hill. Maybe what he'd said was "weather."

"Was that who I think it was?" Alice said, pulling up beside Emily. "I told you we're not too old to go sledding."

"Just let me die," Emily said with annoyance. "You can bury me right here on Pilgrim Hill."

"I don't get it," Alice said. "Weren't you happy to see him?"

❀   ❀   ❀

It started snowing again on the way home. Emily and Alice scaled tall banks on Park Avenue. The neighborhood dogs had begun to leave their mark in the snow-clogged gutters. The driveway at 1163 was filled with snow.

Emily could hear Alice's doorman, Kirk, from the courtyard.

"What good are galoshes if they let in so much water?" he was asking a tall girl in a dripping parka. Her boots left giant puddles over the strip of black rubber leading to the elevator.

"This young lady says she's here to see you," Kirk said as Emily and Alice entered the lobby.

Standing in front of them with her teeth chattering was Phoebe. "H-hi," she said. Scraps of ice dusted her parka and clung to the sprigs of copper hair escaping from under her hood. "My galoshes sprang a leak."

Emily looked down at her red rubber boots. On each, half the toggles were missing.

"What are you waiting for, girls? Take your friend upstairs and run a hot bath," Kirk said.

"I was on my way to school," Phoebe said in the elevator. She pushed her hood back. Her drenched hair clung to her narrow face.

"But didn't you hear that Bromley was closed?" Emily asked. "Just like every other school."

"We don't have a radio," Phoebe said. Alice led her to the bathroom. "That is, we do, but my mother stashed it somewhere when she caught me listening to a rock and roll station the other day. We have a telephone—even my parents admit you can't do without one—but not, heaven forbid, a television set."

She took off her parka and wrung it out over the sink. She pulled off her wet socks. Her toes had turned a purplish blue. "I ran outside in my bathrobe to try to listen to our superintendent's transistor while he shoveled snow. But there was too much static. The anthropology professor across the hall has a radio but he's on sabbatical in Africa. I tried calling Bromley, but all I got was a busy signal. Tons of parents must have been trying to call. Then Philomene said, 'It's just a rinky-dink snowfall and, anyway, don't you have an important science test today?'"

"Yikes!" Emily said. Even Lady Lenore wouldn't have made her travel all the way from the West Side to the East Side in a blizzard if there was the slightest chance school might be closed.

"But you get straight Veegees!" Alice said. "So what if you miss one test?"

"It's just that we couldn't think of a time Bromley had closed because of snow," Phoebe said. "But when I saw those drifts in Riverside Park, I could tell this was no rinky-dink snowfall. When I took Fritz out, he kept collapsing in the snow. I tried calling home from a pay phone on Broadway, but I wasted my only dime on a wrong number. As you know, Emily, my parents don't believe in allowances—they're wasted on candy, they say. They think a bus pass and library card are all I need."

"Well, they can't say you're wasting your money on candy these days!" Emily said.

"I waited and waited for a bus, but no luck," Phoebe continued. "Since the test was going to be first period, I started to walk across the park."

Louisa knelt beside the bathtub and turned the hot water on full blast. "Soak your feet, girl! I'm afraid you got a touch of the frostbite." She stared at Phoebe's bare legs. "My, but you're thin!"

Phoebe dangled her feet in the tub, moaning. "Ouch! I guess toes throb when they thaw out."

"You could have died!" Alice said. "That's what happened to the hero of *Giants in the Earth*." She was talking about a book on Bromley's summer reading list. "Your father's a scientist. Doesn't he know about frostbite?"

Alice had a point. But Phoebe's father was away in the Adirondacks. Phoebe's mother was worried about her watching a few minutes of television, but she didn't worry about her dying of frostbite or pneumonia.

Or of an eating disorder.

"I read that book, too," Phoebe said. "But this is just *frost-nip*. People get it on camping trips. But I knew I couldn't make it all the way to York Avenue in those leaky boots. First my toes felt all tingly, then numb, like when your foot falls asleep. I was near the Ninety-sixth Street exit when it dawned on me that I had friends who live on Ninetieth."

"Friends? I didn't know we were friends anymore," Emily said.

Alice sent her an angry look. "Of course we're friends!"

"Since when are people you're never supposed to visit called friends? We know about the ACGL. We were upstairs at the Peachtree the day Cressida held that meeting. We shouldn't even have let you in the door. Why did you——?"

Alice interrupted. "You're welcome to help yourself to something from my closet, but everything would be swimming on you."

Louisa brought in more towels. Phoebe rubbed her toes dry. "I'll take a look," she said. Emily could hear the clank of hangers against the closet's metal rod.

"What's taking so long?" Alice asked.

"Where's your poodle skirt?" Phoebe asked.

"I don't have one," Alice said.

"And why would you want to wear one of those?" Emily asked. "Aren't they too gaudy for you?"

She couldn't believe what she was saying.

"Yeah, who would want to wear one of those?" Alice quickly said, handing her a kilt. It was too big on Phoebe; it wouldn't stay up. Instead, she put Alice's striped bathrobe back on.

"What size are you anyway?" Alice asked.

"A five, I think."

"That can't be. I'm a seven and you weigh much less than I do."

The phone rang. Alice picked up. It was Emily's mother. "Flora Freund's just called to cancel," she said.

"I'm going to stay at Alice's," Emily said. She sprawled across Alice's bed with the platter of brownies next to her.

Maybe she shouldn't have made that crack about poodle skirts. Not when Phoebe had almost died of frostbite. And why spoil things? She and Phoebe were together and they were having a good time—even if Alice was there. There were a million other things they could talk about: the class dance, posture pictures, Miss Lockwood and Mr. Carslake. Laurence Olivier.

Phoebe broke into Emily's thoughts. "By the way, I think I saw that Rob Gruber or Graybar in the park. The one with the scar. The one you wanted to invite to the dance. He was carrying the lid of a trashcan like a knight's shield."

"You did?" Emily tried to sound bored but her face was on fire. Alice snickered. Emily looked at her menacingly.

"He is kind of cute," Phoebe said.

"Emily's completely gaga over him," Alice said.

Emily heaved a pillow at her. "He's just someone I met at Flora Freund's."

"I don't go to dancing school," Alice said. "That's why I wish Bromley was coed, like the high school in *Rebel Without a Cause,* but with Kensington boys, not juvenile delinquents."

"You saw the movie?" Phoebe asked.

"Yep," Alice said. "I have to admit James Dean was the living end!"

Emily was pretty sure she was lying. Why hadn't she mentioned seeing it before?

"Is the Chicken Run as scary as it sounds?" Phoebe asked. "And does Sal Mineo really kill puppies for fun?"

"My lips are sealed. Do you want me to spoil the movie for you? But we can all go together some time. I don't mind seeing it twice."

"Because you haven't even seen it once!' Emily said. Alice tossed the pillow back. "Can we look at your love magazines?"

"We can look at the few I managed to hide. Mother chucked most of them. She said I was really in for it if she caught me buying them again."

It didn't matter that there weren't new ones, Emily thought, leafing through the October issue of *Modern Romances.* The stories were pretty much the same from month to month. They all had the same basic plot: a boy and girl go steady. They go too far. The girl gets pregnant. The stories were probably based on true incidents.

The names have been changed to protect the innocent.

"The buses are running again," Phoebe said, peering out the window facing downtown. She changed back into her Bromley uniform, which Louisa had put in the dryer. Her boots were still leaking into the pantry sink.

"Here. Try on Bettina's." Alice handed her a pair of tall, shiny black galoshes.

"Is it okay if I return them next weekend?" Phoebe asked. She wasn't about to hand Bettina's boots to Alice at school.

"Don't worry, we won't tell Cressida you were here," Emily said. Phoebe was already halfway out the door. Anyway, shouldn't she just drop the whole thing? She and Phoebe were friends again, sort of, weren't they?

What a good friend would do would try to get her to eat, Emily thought. She handed Phoebe one of Louisa's brownies. "These are the best. They're fudgy, without too many nuts. They're irresistible."

"I'm not hungry."

"You don't have to be hungry to eat this!" But Emily was sure she was hungry. She was always hungry.

"OK, just a taste." Alice broke off a small piece and shoved it in Phoebe's mouth. She swallowed it. A fleeting look of pleasure brightened her gaunt face.

"Come on, that was just a crumb, have some more," Alice said.

"I keep telling you I'm not hungry!" Phoebe said.

19 ❀ In the Cafeteria

"Goody, goody gumdrops!" Alice squealed. She clapped her hands as she inspected the contents of the food cases. "Apple Brown Betty!"

"What's the big deal?" Emily said. Didn't Alice realize how childish she sounded, getting excited about a dumb dessert? But the Brown Betty did look delicious. The food at Bromley was surprisingly tasty. At Great Woods Middle School, lunch was either peanut butter and jelly or SpaghettiOs, with Oreos and canned fruit cocktail or Jell-O for dessert. But at Bromley, you could eat a full meal, like in a restaurant.

Phoebe pushed two trays along the conveyor belt to the hot food section. Emily watched her help herself to cream of tomato soup, roast beef with mashed potatoes, chicken à la king, and a dish of gravy-topped hamburgers called Salisbury Steak. She took a ham sandwich with mayonnaise and a tuna salad plate from the cold food section. From the dessert section, she picked the Brown Betty, a slice of Boston cream pie, a double scoop of vanilla ice cream with butterscotch sauce, tapioca pudding, and two grapefruit halves. The desserts had to go on the second tray.

"I can't believe she's going to eat all that!" Lindsley said before joining the League girls at the table next to Emily's.

"She won't," Margery said. "I think she gets all that food to pad the bill and make her mother believe she eats a lot. I bumped into Mrs. Barrett the other day and she said, 'Margery, Phoebe has lost so much weight. Does she eat normal lunches at school?' I lied. I said yes.'"

Bromley charged no set fee for lunch, and bills varied, depending on the selections. A hot roast beef platter was the most expensive; it cost three dollars. Was Mrs. Barrett, who always tried to save money and sold baby clothes at Best and Co. to meet expenses, so worried about Phoebe's weight loss that she would encourage her to run up an extravagant food bill?

"This is less than usual!" Emily pictured Philomene Barrett saying when last month's bill arrived. "You hardly eat anything for lunch. You're going overboard. Look at yourself. Millie was never this thin. You look like a scarecrow! Don't think I haven't been watching you push the food around your plate at dinner."

And Phoebe would storm out of the kitchen. "I give up! First, I'm too fat, then I'm too thin! There's no way to please you!"

"Take whatever you want," Phoebe said, digging into her grapefruit. "I thought I was hungry, but I'm not. Guess my eyes are too big for my stomach."

"Your stomach isn't big at all!" Holly said, pouncing on the fried chicken while Margery and Lindsley fought over a maraschino cherry on top of the grapefruit.

"Dieting shrinks your stomach," Lindsley said. "You don't have as much room."

Eugenia grabbed the cherry. "It's mine—you promised!"

"I'll take the ice cream," Cressida said. "But next time get chocolate, not butterscotch."

"Butterscotch happens to be my favorite," said Margery.

"Come on, girls, we shouldn't take Phoebe's food," Lindsley said. "We should be encouraging her to eat more." Still, she spooned most of the mashed potatoes on to her plate. "I guess if we don't eat this, it'll only go to waste. I'll take a chicken leg, too—unless of course you change your mind, Pheebs. I'm going to wrap it in a napkin and eat it during study hall. Am I the only one who prefers dark meat?"

"Come on, give me half," Margery said.

"Be my guest." All Phoebe had eaten was the grapefruit. She was excavating its depths, digging through the rind.

"Wish they'd offer us some of that food," Alice said.

"If you need to stuff your face, you can go get your own seconds!" Emily said. On her way out of the cafeteria, she made a point of stopping by the League table. She stared at Phoebe's plate, then at Phoebe. The grapefruit pulp was long gone, and she was sucking on the rind, while the others still gorged on Brown Betty and ice cream.

"Here, want some of this?" Cressida shoved half the ham sandwich practically under Emily's nose. "Or don't you eat pig?"

Phoebe snatched it back. "It's my food. It's not yours to give away."

The Winters were not strictly kosher but they didn't eat pork products. "Thank you," Emily whispered as Phoebe looked away.

20 ❀ A Good Cause

"More recess—that's what I would fight for!" Holly said, pointing emphatically at the ceiling. "We only get ten minutes, which means we have to gobble down our snack too fast, which gives you indigestion, and we don't even have time to pee. Some schools have recess twice a day."

"We'll see if that article of yours proves your case," Miss Heath said with a raspy, wide-mouthed chuckle. Her tongue was tinted green from the Clorets she chewed to mask her tobacco breath.

"All work and no play makes Jane a dull and sickly girl," Margery read from "Longer Recess, Fuller Lives," which she had clipped from *Woman's Home Companion* magazine.

"Interesting perspective," Miss Heath said. She dribbled her stubby fingers across the blotter on her desk. "Although it will take more than that to convince me."

Of all people, Miss Heath should be in favor of extending recess, Emily thought. She'd have more time to puff on her Pall Malls.

Lindsley was next. She read from the *New York Times* article Emily had almost chosen about school segregation in the Deep South. "The poet Carl Sandburg endorses Democratic candidate Adlai Stevenson's pleas for moderation in efforts to integrate the races in Southern public schools."

"Excellent choice," Miss Heath praised.

"But I thought Stevenson was more of a reformer than that," Lindsley said. "The buses in the South were integrated almost as soon as that lady Rosa Parks refused to give up

145

her seat to a white man." She slammed her copy of the *Times* on Miss Heath's desk. "And how come Bromley only has one Negro student?"

If Lindsley was so opposed to prejudice, why did she belong to a club that shunned the Jewish girls? Emily couldn't help wondering.

Miss Heath lifted a pencil to her lips like a cigarette. "Integration and equal rights are valid causes, but we must go slowly with these social changes. At Bromley, as elsewhere, colored people should be eased in gradually."

"What do you mean gradually?" Lindsley asked. "An hour the first day, two hours the second?"

Nervous titters filled the room. "Now, now, sarcasm will get you nowhere, McGovern," Miss Heath chided.

Lindsley lowered her eyes.

Eugenia was next. She read her translation of an article from a Greek newspaper, "Why Everyone Should Study Greek."

"Greek literature is the basis of Western civilization," she began.

"That's just because you know how to speak it already!" Cressida said.

"I know only modern Greek. Ancient Greek is completely different."

"I happen to agree with Stamos," Miss Heath said. "Latin and Greek are the foundations of a modern education. Kaplan, are you ready?"

Barbara had picked an article from the *Herald Tribune*'s Sunday supplement about a campaign to eliminate matrons in movie theaters. Next, Gail read an article from *National Geographic* about the need to preserve endangered animals like the ocelot. Everyone approved.

"It's high time we ended the Cold War!" Alice proclaimed, after reading the article from the *Times* pleading for more cooperation between the United States and the Soviet Union. How much of a teacher's pet could you be? Emily thought.

Everyone knew that the Cold War was Miss Heath's favorite topic.

"Winter, your turn," she said.

The butterflies in Emily's stomach did double flips as she read:

Joanne Donovan, a fourteen-year-old honor student, died of complications from anorexia nervosa yesterday.

Miss Donovan, a freshman at Madison High School, was pronounced dead on arrival at Kings County Hospital at 3:30 in the afternoon. She was rushed to the emergency room when she collapsed in the school gym after displaying signs of light-headedness.

She had been absent from school with the grippe several times this year, reported Madison's principal, Dr. Alan Foster. "Her starvation diet probably lowered her resistance and made her prone to illness."

"Jo was skin and bones," recalled Mrs. Gertrude Schmidt, a neighbor in the Bay Ridge section of Brooklyn. "I tried to get her to try some home-baked chocolate chip cookies but all she would eat was cottage cheese and carrot sticks." At her death, Miss Donovan weighed seventy-four pounds.

Anorexia nervosa, the eating disorder from which Miss Donovan suffered, has been afflicting a growing number of teenage girls, experts say. "Self-starvation is becoming more prevalent as young girls emulate the models in fashion magazines like *Mademoiselle* and *Seventeen,* who are getting thinner and thinner," said Dr. Roger Perry, chairman of King County's department of psychiatry. "The condition, a physical response to psychological conflicts, can dangerously deplete fluid and mineral levels, causing dysmenorrhea, a cessation of menstrual periods, and triggering a potentially fatal electrolyte imbalance."

Calcium and potassium electrolytes are critical for maintaining the electric currents necessary for normal heart function, Dr. Perry said.

"She didn't seem maladjusted until she started that crazy diet," said her best friend and classmate, Nancy Collins.

Miss Donovan's grief-stricken parents could not be reached for comment.

Miss Heath drummed her fingers on her desk. "Please be so good as to explain to the rest of us how this article, interesting as it is, fulfills the assignment."

"Yeah, I don't get it, what would you fight for?" Margery asked.

Emily was stunned. Couldn't they see they had a girl like Joanne Donovan in their midst? She stared directly at Phoebe. It was her first day back after a bout of flu. Like Joanne, she had been out sick often.

Did she realize she was like Joanne? Of course, it was all too easy to choose not to see or hear things you didn't want to. "Hang up your coat!" Lady Lenore yelled every day when Emily tossed it on the settee in the foyer, but she'd learned to let the words waft past her ears like a curl of her father's cigar smoke.

Or the crane at the rubbled construction site outside her bedroom window. At first it had annoyed her. Now she barely noticed it.

And even though Rob had probably completely forgotten that she existed, she could pretend he thought about her all day long.

But Emily's classmates and Miss Heath were even more obtuse. Who cared if you saved the ocelot if you didn't try to save the life of a girl who was dangerously ill?

Maybe the girls in Great Woods were too clothes conscious and boy-crazy, but Emily was pretty sure they would notice a friend who was starving herself to death. She seemed to be the only one making a connection between that article and Phoebe's drastic loss of weight.

"Shouldn't we be on the lookout for something like that anorexia right here at Bromley?" she suggested.

Miss Heath cupped her chin in a veiny, spotted hand.

That's how scrawny Phoebe's hands were beginning to look, without the nicotine stains.

"Bromley prefers to leave medical matters to your families," she said. "Your parents are conscientious; they schedule yearly checkups and consult the doctor when you're sick. Aside from making sure that our students have been vaccinated against smallpox and whooping cough, you might say illness is none of our business except that, of course, we make sure girls who are absent get their books and assignments."

Was turning in assignments on time the only important thing? Even if you were delirious with fever, did you have to find a way to do your homework?

Cressida raised her hand. "Our report isn't supposed to be about a private or personal matter, is it?"

"Exactly," Miss Heath said. "Barrett, you're next."

Slowly, Phoebe made her way to the front of the room.

"Emily's right!" Alice blurted. "Look how skinny she is!"

"Did I call on you, Unger?"

Alice looked down. "Sorry, Miss Heath."

"My report is based on an article from *Foreign Affairs* on the USSR's Five-Year Plans," Phoebe said. "To pursue his idea of collective farming, Joseph Stalin, the ruthless Soviet dictator, seized all private farmland. When the farmers in the Ukraine rebelled, Stalin sold all the wheat grown there to finance his army. This brought about severe famine, in which seven hundred thousand Russians died. It could easily have been avoided, as Stalin had stockpiled enough grain to feed everyone in other parts of the country."

Phoebe went on to read how desperate mothers had tried to throw starving children on to passing trains, hoping passengers would take pity and feed them. By the end of 1933, three million children had perished, Phoebe read.

"Barrett, this is topnotch. I will place it on reserve in the library for all to read," Miss Heath said.

Emily jumped up. "We just heard that millions of people died of hunger during Russia's Five-Year Plans. How can we go on our merry way and pretend not to notice that a classmate is starving herself? Doesn't Bromley care about any-thing but schoolwork? You can't get Veegees if you're dead."

"Winter, this is completely out of line!"

"Look at Phoebe—she might have the same sickness as that Joanne Donovan," Emily continued.

"Emily has a point," Lindsley said.

"No, she doesn't," Phoebe said with surprising emphasis. "The people in Russia were hungry. I'm not."

"You might just have a small stomach," Holly said. "I wish mine was smaller."

"Can we move on to the next report, please?" Phoebe asked.

"Indeed. Whitcroft is next," Miss Heath announced rever-ently, as if she were introducing Eleanor Roosevelt.

"Miss Heath, I'm not feeling well. I'm itchy and I have the chills." Cressida hugged herself to keep warm. "Of course, I did the assignment." She handed Miss Heath a newspaper clipping and several typewritten sheets. "I think I should go see the nurse."

"Very well, Whitcroft, you may present your article next time," Miss Heath said. "Meanwhile, Winter, I suggest you consider choosing another topic. It would be a shame to bring down your average with a Passing Plus."

"I'll stick with this one," Emily said.

21 ❖ Tapestries

By the end of February, more than half the middle school had come down with the German measles. Every day Nurse Lambroza's office was crowded with girls who had taken sick at school.

Miss Heath caught it. Apparently, she'd never had it as a child. Alice and Emily laughed about how there was no point in her getting it since she was way too old to have a baby.

A Bromley-Chatham field hockey tournament had to be cancelled and the seventh grade production of *The Mikado* was postponed. Even the yearly test to measure students' IQs was put off until May.

The ninth-grade field trip to the Cloisters to view the unicorn tapestries had to be postponed, too. Finally, at the end of March, a week before spring vacation, with only a few girls still scratching away at remnants of their rashes, Emily and her classmates boarded the bus for Fort Tryon Park.

Emily had been looking forward to this visit since the beginning of school. With Phoebe, she had pored over pictures of the tapestries, making up stories about the hunters and their ladies and the unicorn. In their version, the unicorn was a family pet, corralled in the backyard of a brownstone, who gamboled with Phoebe's dog, Fritz, in Central Park.

Emily secretly thought her apartment building was more majestic than the Cloisters, even though she knew it was only an imitation of a medieval castle. Anyway, the Cloisters was supposed to look like a monastery, not a castle. Still, she was impressed by the slightly ominous sight of the square stone tower rising above the Hudson River. She could tell that Phoebe, with her nose squashed against the window in the row ahead of her, was impressed, too.

Leading the class past an imposing stone mantle carved with figures of angels and the Virgin Mary, Miss Lockwood came to a stop in front of a tapestry of men in tunics and plumed hats chasing greyhounds through thickly flowering bushes.

"The first tapestry depicts the hunters, "she said. She pointed to a small boy between the trees. "He's giving the signal; the unicorn has been sighted."

Footsteps echoed against the stone floor as the girls moved on to the next tapestry. "And this is where we meet the unicorn," Miss Lockwood said. Milk white with a sprinkling of red freckles and a single spiral horn like a tusk, it rooted around in the ground as if to dig up precious metals.

"Ooh, it's so cute," Holly said. "Do they sell toy unicorns in the gift shop?"

Miss Lockwood ignored her. "As a mythical creature, the unicorn was a symbol. One theory is romantic: The bloodstains were wounds inflicted by a lover's arrow. Is the unicorn akin to a bridegroom, hunted down by his lady, a victim of the vicissitudes of courtship, as it were, a captive to Eros, to passion?" She asked with a hint of excitement.

"What's a 'vissitude'?" Holly asked.

"Vicissitude," Miss Lockwood corrected. "A variation in fortune, the ups and downs of life, as it were. Is anyone keeping track of Nifties?"

"I am!" Everyone shouted, whipping out notebooks and pens. Emily jotted down "Eros."

"The unicorn could be a she—a bride all dressed in white," Alice suggested. "Captive to one of those cute guys in the tights."

Emily batted her eyelashes. "Katie's the one who's captive to a certain creature, as it were. Subtle hint: he's our only male teacher."

In the next tapestry, the unicorn poked his horn in a stream of water gushing from a fountain.

"Ick, it's got drops of blood all over it!" Holly said. "Those poor women who spent their days embroidering this—they must have pricked themselves!"

"Ah, you make the common mistake of assuming the weavers were women. In the Middle Ages, unlikely as it may seem, they were mostly men," Miss Lockwood said.

"Why not? My father's a surgeon," Gail said. "He knows how to stitch and sew. And how could those possibly be bloodstains? Real blood wouldn't stay red after so many centuries. We learned about oxidation in biology. When blood hits the air, it turns brown."

We didn't need biology class for that, Emily felt like saying. Getting your period made this clear.

"Gail is right. Those are meant to be drops of juice from the pomegranate tree; they were made with vermilion thread and deliberately woven into the tapestry," Miss Lockwood said.

Lady Lenore was in the process of needlepointing a clown pillow for Evan's crib. There was no special skill to it. All she had to do was follow ready-made outlines with the colors painted in.

"The other interpretation is religious: The unicorn's capture is a symbol of Jesus Christ's suffering, crucifixion, and resurrection," Miss Lockwood said.

"So the hunters are persecuting the unicorn like Jesus's enemies persecuted him," Cressida said. "But he's turning the other cheek."

"Astutely observed, Cressida. And notice that after the unicorn dips its purifying horn in the water, as it were, the birds and wild beasts, creatures who figure prominently in medieval poetry, are able to drink from the fountain again."

"And before that they couldn't because the water was poisoned, right?" Cressida asked.

"In the sense that the medieval world hadn't yet discovered how to keep harmful microbes away," Miss Lockwood said. "Rather, I would say it was poison*ous*. Indeed, controlling the bacteria in our water supply has been one of the crowning achievements of our century, as it were."

"In Greece, tap water still makes you sick. You have to boil it. We drink mineral water when we're there," Eugenia said.

"But, Miss Lockwood, wasn't poison in the form of bacteria added to the water in the wells on purpose?" Cressida said.

Below the Cloisters, the Hudson River floated by, icy and forbidding like a moat. It was polluted, Emily knew, unsuitable for swimming or drinking, but no one ever suggested that bacteria had been dumped into it on purpose.

"More often people claimed that snake venom was responsible," Miss Lockwood said, "but there were other theories."

She was interrupted by strains of music from the entryway. A trio of musicians in jesters' caps skipped into the tapestry hall, strumming a lute and mandolin and what Emily now recognized as a rebec.

"Al—Mr. Carslake, I didn't know this was one of your concert days!" Miss Lockwood said.

"We're here every Thursday, Ka—Miss Lockwood." Mr. Carslake doffed his royal blue cap. "Don't you know that we also serve as the Cloisters' resident early music group?"

"She knows, all right," Alice whispered.

"She's turning as red as the unicorn's pomegranate!" Emily whispered back.

"Emily," Miss Lockwood said, looking stern. "Perhaps you have something of interest to share concerning the unicorn?"

"Uh, no, not really. I was just thinking about *The Court Jester*," Emily lied. Instead, she was thinking about what Cressida had said.

"Might you be referring to me or to a member of my troupe?" Mr. Carslake asked, nodding in the musicians' direction.

"I meant the movie with Danny Kaye," Emily said.

"A movie? A motion picture? How charming!" Mr. Carslake said. The bells on his cap tinkled as he led his troupe out.

Miss Lockwood followed him. "Girls, why don't you go have a look at the garden?" she said.

"I bet he's going to sing her an oh-bad!" Alice said as Miss

Lockwood and Mr. Carslake walked into a chapel dominated by a huge crucifix. "Maybe this is where they'll tie the knot!"

Miss Lockwood had said that in a few weeks the cloister garden would flower with Lady's mantle, St. John's wort, hollyhock, and other herbal plants, which medieval monks believed could cure the common cold and keep elves and goblins at bay. But with the air still frosty, the only green to be seen was on the fir trees bordering the garden and the leaves of potted plants set along the parapet.

Emily zipped up her parka and drew it tightly around her, but she couldn't stop shivering. Cressida's comments had unnerved her.

"How come you never caught the German measles?" Cressida asked Alice, fixing her with a steely gaze. Despite her efforts to catch the disease, Alice had stayed healthy.

"I tried! I spent the whole afternoon with Emily while she was sick!" Alice said. "Maybe I have a natural immunity."

Cressida turned to Emily. "And you! Even though you were the first, you had such a mild case. Out for only a day, and when you came back, hardly a mark—almost as if you'd never had it at all." Her own face still showed the ghost of a rash. She'd missed three whole days of school.

"The doctor said I had a perfect case. He came over to study it," said Emily. "Straight from a textbook, he said!" She still got the chills when she thought of Dr. Nat inspecting her rash. Just the other day she'd spotted him in the neighborhood, too far away to say hi, darting into an apartment building with his doctor's bag.

"I still say it's strange that a certain group of girls didn't catch the German measles when pretty much everyone else did," Cressida said.

"Yeah, Barbara and Gail didn't catch it either, did they?" Margery asked.

"Yeah, none of the other Clothes Girls got the German measles," Eugenia said.

"The clothes *who?*" Gail asked.

Emily and Alice locked eyes.

"I already had the German measles," Barbara said. "In first grade."

"What's the big deal? It's not polio!" Phoebe said. Her shoulders sloped forward. She looked exhausted. "Besides, Emily did us a favor. It's important to develop an immunity to rubella before you get married and have children. When I woke up with a rash last week, my mother said she would make me go to school and spread the germs around except that I had probably already done so already because you're contagious the day before, so she let me stay home."

"It's just that the whole thing reminds me of the Middle Ages," Cressida said.

Miss Lockwood joined them in the garden. "It always warms my heart to hear discussions about your studies beyond the classroom. But what is it that once again prompts my Bromley girls to draw connections, as it were, between contemporary events and those of a bygone era?"

"I know that in the fourteenth century the Black Plague spread like wildfire and a certain group of people was accused of poisoning the wells because they were just about the only ones who didn't get it. So I think it's fishy the way this German measles epidemic affected the whole school except for certain girls," Cressida said.

Emily had heard about how the Jews had been accused of poisoning the water with the germs that spread the Black Plague.

"The Plague or Black Death, which was caused by rat bites, felled nearly half of Europe; German measles, or rubella, is a perfectly ordinary childhood disease," Miss Lockwood said. "Are you insinuating that some of your classmates contaminated Bromley's water supply with germs?"

No one answered.

"I'm asking you a question, Cressida," Miss Lockwood said.

Phoebe looked up, eyes wide. Alice poked Emily in the ribs. The only sound was the clicking of a guard's heels as he patrolled the tapestry hall.

"Not the water supply, but the punch bowl at the class dance," Cressida said after a long pause. "Someone's date had a flask. He could have spiked the punch with germs."

Normally the idea of Davy hatching such a scheme would have Emily laughing her head off. Instead, she was shaking. Trying to spike the punch with whiskey was bad enough; mixing in germs, even ones that weren't fatal, was much worse.

"That's preposterous!" Miss Lockwood said. "I would rather not attribute any malice to your allegations. I prefer to believe that your imagination has been running away with you."

"I'm not saying it happened for sure. I'm saying it's possible, that's all," Cressida said.

"Somebody really good in science could figure out how," said Margery.

"Once my cousin mashed up aspirin and mixed it in my Coke to get me drunk," Holly said.

Miss Lockwood buttoned her tweed storm coat and pulled her purple beret over her ears. "Girls, I think we'd better leave."

"But we haven't discussed *The Unicorn in Captivity*," Alice said. The final tapestry showed the unicorn grazing in a fence-like enclosure, safe from the hunters but free to roam.

"And what about the tapestry where a virgin subdues it?" Eugenia said. "Only a virgin had those powers."

Uneasy titters followed.

The unicorn is like most of us, Emily thought, ordinary except maybe for a single trait that makes us different or special. We're all hemmed in by our appearance and personality and by people who push us around, if we allow ourselves to be.

"And Whitcroft, I want to speak to you privately in the homeroom as soon as we get back," Miss Lockwood said.

It was the first time Emily had heard her address any of them by their last name.

"We have yearbook pictures!" Cressida protested.

"I'm afraid they'll have to be taken without you. They print an 'absent' list, do they not?"

Emily had never heard Miss Lockwood sound sarcastic before. "Everybody on the bus immediately!" she ordered.

"Can't we go to the gift shop?" Holly whined.

22 ❀ Loose Change

"The period between 1000 AD and the Renaissance was an era of heightened religious devotion, which, at times, bordered on the fanatic," Miss Lockwood said. She stood next to the bus driver like a tour guide. "This fervor, as it were, was expressed in glorious art and architecture and literature. Alas, it also led to the targeting of scapegoats when things went wrong." She paused. "Someone remember to put 'scapegoats' in the Nifties."

Notebooks and pencils were whipped out. "Often, Jewish people were unfairly blamed for such scourges because they worshiped in their own language and ate different foods and lived in their own villages, apart from the Christian community."

"See, things are different for Jewish people now," Alice whispered as the bus hurtled down Fifth Avenue.

"May I remind you of something called the Anti–Clothes Girl League?" Emily said. "And what about what happened to Anne Frank and millions of other Jewish people in World War II?"

But Alice was scratching her face. "I don't know what's wrong with me. All of a sudden I feel really sick."

Tiny pink circles dotted her forehead and cheeks. "Alice has the German measles!" Emily shouted.

"Hooray!" Alice said with a wide grin. Even her braces seemed to sparkle.

"How lucky can you get?" Emily said with a sigh of relief.

"Alice, check in with Nurse Lambroza as soon as we get back to school," said Miss Lockwood.

In the Bromley vestiary, combs, compacts and tubes of Tangee were passed from girl to girl. Headbands were straightened and pageboys tucked under.

Alice wasn't there; she had been sent home by Nurse Lambroza. "Just as well," she told Emily before leaving. "I wouldn't want my rash in the picture."

The school photographer, Mr. Lambroza, who was Nurse Lambroza's husband, divided the ninth graders into four rows. The tallest girls, like Margery and Phoebe, stood in the back under a painting of the East River. The rest were supposed to stand in the next two rows or sit in front on the oriental carpet, with legs folded neatly to the side in the same direction, to the left or right of the class president. She was supposed to hold up the class mascot, which was a stuffed animal of Eeyore from *Winnie-the-Pooh*.

But Eeyore lolled forlornly on the rug.

Lindsley grabbed him. She was class vice president. "Cressida is meeting with Miss Lockwood."

Just then, though, Cressida burst into the vestiary. "Perfect timing!" She said breathlessly. She snatched Eeyore from Lindsley's lap, plunked herself down in the middle of the first row, and said, "Mr. Lambroza, you can take our picture now."

Instead, Mr. Lambroza ran up to Phoebe and shouted, "Put your head between your legs!"

Phoebe had keeled over, toppling Margery and Gail in the third row and the girls in the second row until they collapsed like a stack of dominoes. She landed on her back in front of Cressida, unconscious.

"She looks dead!" Cressida screamed. Everybody screamed.

A coin rolled down, stopping at Emily's feet. It was the dime that Phoebe got instead of a real allowance, ten cents for an emergency phone call. Emily rushed to the phone booth in the corner of the vestiary.

She dialed the operator. "We need an ambulance!" She screamed. "570 East Eighty-second Street!"

She had used that phone only once before, after getting a Passing Minus on an algebra test. No one had answered, not even Fräulein or Harriet, and her dime had come rolling back.

Within minutes a series of waa-waas sounded and a red and white ambulance pulled up in front of the school.

23 ❀ A Joint Assignment

During homeroom the next morning, Miss Lockwood told the class about Phoebe. She had been taken to Doctors' Hospital a block away, in an unconscious state induced by malnourishment and she was being fed intravenously.

Suppose she never woke up? As far as Emily knew, people awakened from comas only in science fiction books. What if she died like that poor Joanne Donovan? What if she died because no one at Bromley had paid attention to that article or because people swiped her food instead of trying to get her to eat? Or because her teachers didn't notice that she was starving?

"That way she'll get enough nourishment," Miss Lockwood said. But would it be enough to make her conscious again? Emily wondered. "I'll let you know as soon as visiting is permitted. Meanwhile, there will be no further disruption of your studies. As you know, history term papers are due a week before Easter vacation. Has everyone's topic been approved?"

Miss Lockwood had approved Emily's topic, "The Birth of the Hanseatic League," but she had another idea. She raised her hand. "Miss Lockwood, I'd like to change my topic, if that's okay."

"Why? The Hanseatic League is a perfectly reasonable choice."

"Anyone can do it. I'd rather write a paper about Jews in the Middle Ages."

You could have heard a paper clip drop.

163

"Very well," Miss Lockwood said after a moment's thought. "But I have another idea. Though it is my preference to have students choose their own topic and work individually, I will make one exception this year." She took a deep breath. "Cressida will collaborate with Emily on a paper about medieval anti-Semitism."

Emily collaborate with Cressida? Was she serious?

"Emily and Cressida?" Lindsley said incredulously.

"Anti-whatsis?" Margery asked.

"I know what that is! Prejudice against people who are Jewish," Gail said.

"Like the Anti–Clothes Girl League!" said Holly.

Cressida shot her a murderous look. "Miss Lockwood, it's not fair! I already started taking notes for my paper on heraldry and the Whitcroft coat of arms."

"Quiet, please!" Miss Lockwood said. Her voice vibrated with anger. "I'm afraid this is a required assignment, not an elective project."

"Can I collaborate?" Lindsley cried out. "I think you need more than two people for a project like this."

"Pretty please, me, too!" Margery pleaded.

"What about me? After all, I'm Jewish even if I don't go to temple!" Alice said.

"My uncle's wife is half Jewish!" said Holly.

"I think I should help, too! My parents are opposed to all forms of discrimination and bigotry," said Lindsley.

"Mine, too!" said Margery. "At least I think they are."

"I know about prejudice. Some people are prejudiced against Greek people," Eugenia said.

What a pack of followers, Emily thought. How fickle could you be? Only a short time ago they had gone along with Cressida to form a club to ostracize the Jewish girls. Now they wanted to write a paper with them. Maybe it was because their snub had never been more than a pose, a game of follow-the-leader. Maybe they'd never really had their hearts in it. Maybe their new friendliness wasn't sincere, either.

Any of you are welcome to work with Cressida instead of

me, Emily felt like saying. At one point, she had to admit, there might have been something thrilling about working with Cressida—to have a chance to study her every move and figure out what made her the way she was. There was nothing wrong with imitating someone you admired. But, apart from her looks, Emily had never admired Cressida. She had envied her, which wasn't the same thing.

"You are all free to help, as long as you work on your own papers as well," Miss Lockwood continued, "but only Emily and Cressida can turn in a paper on this particular subject."

"I don't see why one of the others can't do it instead of me," Cressida muttered.

"I, for one, withdraw my offer to help," Alice said. "I can't work on two papers!"

"I am not finished with what I have to say," Miss Lockwood said. "There will be another field trip, as it were: You are all to go see the award-winning Broadway show, *The Diary of Anne Frank,* about anti-Semitism during World War II. Bromley will order a block of tickets."

"Goody, goody!" Alice said. "I'm dying to see it again!"

"Me, too!" Emily said.

"I feel so sorry for you," Alice said later. She still felt sick. She'd had one of the worst cases of rubella Dr. Sturges had ever seen, she told Emily. "Collaborating with Cressida, I mean."

"It's probably worse for her than for me. And it's not as if it's somebody dumb like Holly. After all, Cressida does get her share of Veegees."

They would have to start working together soon, Emily realized. She screwed up her courage and asked Cressida if she would be free sometime over the weekend.

"I'll have to see," Cressida said. "Maybe Sunday after church."

24 ❀ Coordinated Outfits

"I haven't actually seen you and Cressida together," Alice commented. "Seems to me you've been working on your lonesome."

"We do it by phone, mostly," Emily said. She had lent Cressida one of her father's Jewish history books so that she could do her research separately.

Eventually, though, there was no way out of it: Emily and Cressida had to meet in the reading room at the main branch of the New York Public Library to take notes from the Jewish Encyclopedia.

"Meet you in the Rotunda," Cressida said. She didn't suggest they go downtown together. On the crowded Fifth Avenue bus, Emily's hand shook, along with the strap it was hanging from. The butterflies were doing somersaults. She had never been alone with Cressida before.

She ran up the stairs, between the giant lion statues, and pushed through the swinging doors into the circular space known as the Rotunda. She felt tiny amid the tall, gilded arches and frescoed ceilings as high as the sky. She checked her watch. Cressida was late. Had she made a mistake? Were they supposed to meet in the main reading room instead? Patches of perspiration spread under her arms. Had she forgotten to put on deodorant?

Cressida wasn't even out of breath when she arrived fifteen minutes later without so much as a "sorry." "Let's go," she said brusquely. Emily followed her into the reading room. They were the only non-grown-ups there. Cressida picked a seat with a man and a woman on either side. A jacket was draped over the chair directly opposite her, so Emily sat on the one next to it. Facing her was a stocky man with a brush-like mustache, perusing an Atlas.

At the reference desk, Emily asked for the C and I volumes of the encyclopedia, the ones that would have articles on the Crusades and the Inquisition. She picked volume C–D and Cressida chose Volume H–I. No talking was allowed, so they took notes in silence and jotted down questions on index cards and passed them back and forth.

With horror, Emily read about a massacre in Germany in which women and children had been murdered. She wasn't sorry she hadn't been born in the Middle Ages. It was obvious there'd been more bloodshed than romance. Of course, in this century, there had been the Nazis. And at Bromley, though a comparison seemed extreme, there was the Anti–Clothes Girls League.

Emily couldn't help noticing how jumpy Cressida seemed. She kept gripping her hair in a ponytail and twisting a rubber band around it, then releasing it. Would a truly self-confident person do that? Maybe she was more insecure than people realized.

By the time Emily and Cressida had accumulated a stack of 3 × 5 index cards, the library was ready to close. They were the only people left at their table.

"Why don't you come to my house?" Cressida said. "We'll organize our research." It made sense. They didn't have much time. The paper was due in two weeks.

"You know the Crusades weren't really against Jewish people," Cressida said as they skipped down the library steps. "They were against the Muslims. The Christians wanted to reclaim Jerusalem."

"I don't see why that's any better," Emily said. "Why should the Christians have been against anyone?"

Cressida lived in a penthouse on Fifth Avenue. The living room was as grand as Phoebe's was shabby. From the terrace, which was covered with plants, you could see across the park to the tall apartment buildings on Central Park West.

On a glass coffee table, art books were arranged in neat piles. A silver lighter shaped like Aladdin's lamp stood next to a crystal dish filled with different brands of cigarettes—some with filters, some without.

Cressida picked a Winston. Miss Lockwood had told the class never to smoke that brand because of a grammatical error in their ad: "Winstons taste good like a cigarette should."

"It should be, as a cigarette should," she said.

"Like I give a damn what that loon Lockwood told us," Cressida said, as if reading Emily's mind. "I mean, as if I should give a damn." She blew out perfectly formed smoke rings as she led Emily to her room. Emily could tell she had been smoking for some time.

"See this chart?" Cressida said. Emily wasn't prepared for the messy piles of paper and clothing scattered across the floor. Clearing a path through the clutter, Cressida pushed a large slab of poster board subdivided into calendar squares across the floor. "I'm going to a different school next year. A boarding school. Amber Hill. Isn't that a pretty name? It's coed and there's no uniform. So my wardrobe will be especially important."

"How come?" Emily asked. Amber Hill. It sounded familiar.

"Mother thinks Bromley isn't as rigorous as it used to be."

Her mother wanted to send her to boarding school because she was always traveling, Emily figured. She felt a flicker of pity for Cressida.

"I'm coordinating combinations of separates for the first thirty days, taking the weather into account, of course. I'm determined not to repeat the same outfit for at least a month. Of course, I'll be getting some new clothes, but I have to wait for the August issue of *Glamour* to come out."

The first entry, written in perfect Bromley block letters, was dated September 14, 1956, the day Amber Hill presumably began:

～ Indian summer: sleeveless McMullen blouse with accordion-pleated loden green skirt & beige Villager cable-knit cardigan tied around waist.

～ Autumn chill: coral sweater-set with tweed straight skirt with pinkish tones or with charcoal gray Bermuda shorts for informal social events.

～ Orientation: baby-blue turtleneck and black-watch plaid kilt maybe with the kind of black tights Miss Lockwood wears.

～ First day of classes: slacks, preferably gray flannel (check Best & Co.!!!) and mint-green, Oxford-cloth button-down shirt under crewneck pullover.

～ First dance: new poodle skirt with black kid ballet flats.

A sketch of a circle skirt with a curly-haired dog on it accompanied the last entry.

"So what do you think?" Cressida asked anxiously. She held up a black felt skirt embossed with a silver poodle. "You can touch it! It won't bite! Mother doesn't know I bought it. She thinks poodle skirts are cheap looking."

The smile faded. "You've got to help me, I'm desperate! No matter how many outfits I come up with, there's always one duplication," she moaned. "See!" She pointed to a week at the end of October in which the same beige Shetland crewneck sweater appeared twice. "There has to be one more new combination, there just has to!"

Her even features had contorted into a grimace. She didn't look like the class beauty. She didn't look like the co-captain of the hockey team. She didn't look like the president of the dance committee. She didn't look like Carol Lynley.

"Can't you think of anything?" she pleaded.

"I don't think it matters if you repeat an outfit," Emily said. "Besides, you said you'll be getting new clothes, so that should solve the problem."

"A great help you are!" Cressida took off the poodle skirt and hurled it across the room. It landed with the poodle's rhinestone eye glaring glassily at Emily like the eye of a dead fish.

Emily called Alice as soon as she got home. "Did you know that Cressida is going to boarding school next year? A place I never heard of—Amber Hill. It's coed."

"You're kidding! You never heard of Amber Hill? It's a special school. A school for troubled teenagers. I think they have psychoanalysts there. "

Cressida Whitcroft at a school for teens with problems? It was hard to imagine. Cressida flinging clothes across the floor was hard to imagine, too. A school with psychoanalysts might not be such a bad idea, Emily thought.

For now, though, she wondered how she and Cressida would ever finish their paper.

25 ❀ Flannel Robes

In school the next day, Cressida acted as if nothing had happened. Her face had resumed its usual air of composure. There was nothing to remind Emily of the crazed girl flinging clothes across the floor.

When classes were over, they met in a French classroom festooned with posters of the Eiffel Tower and the Louvre. Cressida was calm as they divided the paper into sections on the Crusades, the Black Plague, and the Spanish Inquisition. Cressida informed Emily that her new stepfather's secretary planned to type her sections of the paper on a new electric typewriter in his law office.

"Cressida's sections will look so much better than mine," Emily complained at dinner later. That's all her father had to hear. "Want to make a bet?" he said. The next day he brought home an IBM electric typewriter and a box of 100 percent corrasable bond paper. "This is better than your friend's. It's the very latest model."

What a copycat! Yet at a recent office appliances convention he had been called a leader in his field.

But when Emily pressed the letters on the white keyboard, her fingers ran away with her. If she touched the A, a whole string of As showed up. What was she thinking? She had never even typed on a regular typewriter before.

"Your mother can do it," her father said. "She was the world's greatest secretary!"

But the world's greatest secretary had no better luck.

When Lady Lenore tapped the keys, they flew away from her. She unplugged the IBM and glared at Lord Sidney. "You and your crazy contraptions!"

Finally, it was the night before the paper was due. Emily hadn't finished a day too soon. Her rough draft took up eleven single-spaced foolscap pages. She would have to recopy it by hand. To write legibly would take forever. Cressida's contribution would look so much better, typed by a professional.

Emily could feel her mother's eyes on her as she loaded her fountain pen with India ink. The last thing she needed was for Lady Lenore to watch as she wrote. To her relief, she left the room.

She came back, lugging a square leather case, and set it on the table. She fiddled with the latch. "The least you could do is give me a hand, Sidney!"

Emily's father pulled out a portable Remington typewriter with a plastic cover over it. Her mother removed the cover. She sat down, staring at the black and white keyboard.

"I'll probably be a little rusty. I haven't used this in years. I'll need a few minutes to brush up."

"Typing's like riding a bike—you never forget how," Lord Sidney said.

She inserted a sheet of paper behind the roller, then curled her fingers over the top row and very slowly tapped out the letters Q W E R T Y U I O P. She moved to the middle row and placed the fingers of her left hand on A S D F and her right fingers on J K L and the key with the semicolon on it.

"This is called the home position. You keep your fingers poised over these keys and move up and down and to the left and right," she said.

Emily liked that: the home position.

"Give it a try," her mother said. But it took Emily forever just to type the title. She got every other letter wrong. Her gummy eraser left smudges. By the time she reached the word "Inquisition," it was already 8:15. At this rate, it would take her all night. It wasn't her fault, she told herself. It wasn't as if she'd gone to secretarial school.

"Forget the home position," her father said. "Use the old hunt-and-peck method like a reporter. That's how I typed my assignments in night school."

"Let me help," her mother said.

Let me help? Did Lady Lenore, Mrs. Sidney H. Winter, actually utter those words? Did she mean she would type it? It couldn't be coming from the goodness of her heart, Emily told herself; it was just that she took pride in her secretarial skills. But Emily wasn't about to turn down the offer.

She handed over her rough draft. Her mother inserted a fresh page. She made three mistakes in the first paragraph alone. She certainly wasn't the crack typist Emily had been led to believe, even when she used her own typewriter. Nothing like Ann Sothern on *Private Secretary*. Of course, that was just a television program and, for all Emily knew, Ann Sothern had clacked away at any old keys.

Her mother was picking up speed. "Meanwhile, you could put in the illustrations and proofread as I finish each page," she suggested.

Emily daubed rubber cement over the back of a tracing from the encyclopedia of crusaders attacking a Jewish village in France and pasted it on her title page. She rubbed away the bits of rubber cement pills that collected outside the borders of the pictures.

"Appalling," her mother muttered as she typed verses from "The Prioress's Tale" by Geoffrey Chaucer, in which a Jew was blamed for the murder of a Christian boy. The ninth grade was going to read *The Canterbury Tales* after spring vacation.

She got up and stretched. "I'm going to change into something more comfortable." She looked silly all right, typing at the kitchen table in her turquoise silk hostess gown. Emily half expected her to put on the kind of skirt and blouse Ann Sothern wore to the office, but she came back in a plaid flannel bathrobe Emily had never seen her wear before.

A flannel bathrobe. And a ratty one at that.

Emily went into her room and took off her Bromley uniform. She put on her own plaid flannel robe.

Her mother's long nails made a racket, and, occasionally, she had trouble deciphering Emily's handwriting, and Emily's eyes fogged over as she checked each finished page, but most of the time, they made a team.

"This story scared me to death when I was your age," her mother said as she typed a quotation from "The Pit and the Pendulum" by Edgar Allan Poe, which took place during the Inquisition. Had she read it at her public school in the Bronx? Emily definitely didn't know everything there was to know about her mother.

Most of the time, she seemed to be concentrating too hard on the mechanics of typing to comment on what Emily had written. Couldn't she say something nice about the paper itself?

As the clock in the foyer chimed twelve times, Fräulein appeared in the doorway, still in her white uniform. "Ah!" she said with a smile so wide you could see the gold fillings clumped in the back of her mouth. "This is a sight for, how you are saying it, eyes that are hurting."

That was not how you say it, but Emily was too tired to correct her.

"You're up late, Fräulein," her mother said with a sigh. "I guess that means Evan woke up for a bottle."

"No, not yet," Fräulein said. She was still smiling as she walked back to the nursery.

"That's a powerful paper, Emily," her mother said as they stumbled off to bed at 2:36. "Truly exceptional."

"Did you hear what Mom said?" Emily whispered to Scottie under the covers. "That compliment came from not only her heart, but from her brain, too!"

Mom! Suddenly, it sounded right.

"Twizzle, you and your mother almost pulled an all-nighter," Emily's father said a few hours later as Emily yawned her way through breakfast. "Knock, knock."

"Not now, Sidney, we're too pooped," her mother said. To wake Emily up, she made her drink a cup of instant coffee.

Fräulein walked in, holding the Blob high, like a trophy.

"Sir Evan has slept through the night!" she said triumphantly. She handed him to his mother.

"Well, it's about time. But he has to do it a few nights in a row before we declare victory."

"Ah, but this was already the second time." So Fräulein had known about that other night.

The phone rang. Fräulein rushed to pick it up. "Congratulations!" she said. "8½ pounds—such a big girl!" Then, "I will be there by noon *punkt*." She hung up.

Lady Lenore looked startled. "Did I hear what I think I heard?"

"Today I start with another newborn," Fräulein said.

"Today? In just a few hours? It's not right to give us so little notice!"

"My dear Frau Winter, I always said I would leave once Evan slept through the night. I never stay with a family longer than that. Never did I give you any false impression. And now my new baby has been born!"

"I don't care. This is much too abrupt, Fräulein. Evan is barely three months old. Suppose those two nights he slept through were a fluke?"

"If you could stay up typing Emily's paper you can stay up with Evan, if necessary," Fräulein said. "Of course, you could use a little more practice handling him."

That was putting it mildly, Emily thought as she followed Fräulein into the nursery. For once, she agreed with her mother, though. Fräulein owed them more than a few hours' warning, she thought as she watched her drag out the same battered suitcase with the peeling steamship stickers that she had unpacked three months earlier. She watched her fold in her three white uniforms and the two white cardigans. She watched her tuck into a plastic bag the package of hairpins, the Orange Flame lipstick and nail polish, the hair net, and the half-empty bottle of mineral oil. She threw out the bottle of hair dye; it was all used up.

When Fräulein left the room for a minute, Emily slipped in the marble heart. She had glued it together unevenly, but

Fräulein didn't deserve even a broken gift for taking off with so little notice. Did she have to leave in such a hurry?

Her mother came in, carrying Evan at arm's length. "He has a dirty diaper," she said, lowering him onto the changing table. "The least you can do is change him one last time."

Fräulein washed Evan off and sprinkled baby powder over his spongy pink bottom. She pinned on a diaper and pulled up a pair of rubber pants. Then, holding him close in the rocking chair, she gave him his morning apple juice bottle. Was it really for the last time?

"You will help your mother, Emily, *ja?*"

"I go to school every day, remember? In fact, I'm already late! What about Harriet?" It was terrifying to think of her mother alone with Evan but there was no way Emily could take on all of Fräulein's responsibilities. Never become too attached, Fräulein had said. But she'd made sure Emily became attached to Evan and to her.

"The diaper service delivers every Thursday," Fräulein said. "And there's plenty of corn syrup and Carnation for formula. Harriet knows how to mix it, if you have any questions."

If they had questions? They would have millions of them. And what about *Queen for a Day?* What about *Dragnet?* What about *The Big Surprise* and *The $64,000 Question?* Would the next family own a television set? Would there be a teenage girl to watch it with?

Would Fräulein miss her?

"My job is done," she announced, sounding satisfied. Tears welled up as Emily ran over to hug her. Fräulein hugged her back, then gently pushed her away. She put on her muskrat coat, even though it was getting too warm for fur, picked up her battered suitcase and, quicker than you could say *The Big Surprise,* Fräulein Hilda Wertheimer was out the door.

26 ❖ More Poodle Skirts

Miss Lockwood was so impressed with Emily and Cressida's paper that she showed it to Miss Foxworthy. Old Foxy, in turn, was so impressed that she called Emily and Cressida into her office for a private meeting.

"This is a scholarly, balanced approach to a sensitive topic," she said in her most serious and solemn voice. "It deserves a wide audience." And there was only one way to guarantee that: a Special Assembly.

And that's how Emily and Cressida—Winter and Whitcroft!—found themselves sharing the assembly hall podium a few days before spring vacation. From that podium, Miss Foxworthy had consoled the James Dean mourners, read parables from the Bible and lectured on the importance of posture pictures. Now two ninth graders would be presenting a term paper about Jews.

Officially, it was called the Anti-Prejudice Assembly. Unofficially, it would be known as the Poodle Skirt Assembly.

Students were allowed out of uniform for the occasion, and everyone in the League—the ex-League, that is—had agreed to wear a circle skirt. Lindsley had pinned a snow-white unicorn made of felt on a velvet skirt. Holly's skirt had an angora kitten on it. Eugenia's was pink with a poodle on a sequined leash. Margery had found a felt skirt with two poodles, one black and one white, at the Bromley-Chatham Exchange. Cressida wore her felt skirt with the silver poodle. Emily wore her Scottie skirt.

Phoebe was still in the hospital, attached to an IV. She had regained consciousness, Miss Lockwood announced that morning. Emily planned to visit her right after the assembly.

Crowds streamed into the assembly hall. The entire upper school and their teachers were there. Parents had been invited and ninth graders could invite guests. Emily tried to ignore the blur of faces in front of her as she recited the first paragraph from memory:

"The Middle Ages was not only the age of chivalry and the feudal system. It was a time of extreme religious zeal when the twin ogres of intolerance and fanaticism invaded Europe. In the first century AD, during the emperor Nero's reign, the Romans threw Christians to the lions in the Colosseum," she said, projecting her voice as loudly as she could. "It was a sport; spectators cheered. But by the Middle Ages, most of Europe had turned Catholic. People forgot that Pontius Pilate, a Roman prefect, had sentenced Jesus Christ to death, and now they blamed his crucifixion mainly on the Jews."

Emily stepped aside to let Cressida take over. Her voice was steady as she read, "In 1096, Pope Urban II called for an armed Crusade to capture the Holy Land from the Muslims, or Mohammedans. They were known as infidels because they didn't practice Christianity. On their way to the Middle East, the crusaders figured, 'Why not get rid of the Jews? They're not Christian, either.' Once they made it to Jerusalem, the Crusaders crushed the city's inhabitants. Jews and Muslims fought together to defend the city but didn't stand a chance against the Crusaders with their lances and crossbows."

Emily sneaked a look at the audience. That mass of dark green in the back row—were those Kensington blazers? She had no idea boys' schools had been invited. Was Rob there?

To think she'd been wearing her glasses the whole time, even for the part she had memorized! She couldn't take them off now. She didn't know the rest by heart. And it was her turn again.

Cressida stepped aside—a little slowly, in Emily's opinion. "The enemy showed no mercy for babes and sucklings, no pity for women about to give birth," Emily read from an account by a nameless Jew, who recorded how marauding bands of crusaders attacked Jewish communities along the Rhine River. "Local priests had tried to protect the Jews, but they, too, were beaten or killed."

Emily felt uncomfortable standing next to Cressida. Her mother would be comparing them and wishing Emily had Cressida's willowy figure and perfect pageboy and eyes that could see without glasses.

It bothered Emily that writing this paper might seem like Cressida's choice. No one outside their class would realize that Cressida had wanted to write about her family's coat of arms, which just happened to date back to the Crusades.

It was Cressida's turn again. "And, as if the Crusades weren't enough, in 1290, all the Jews were expelled from England for practicing usury," she read. "This means they were lending money and charging interest, which Christians were not allowed to do. It wasn't fair to punish the Jews for doing this since it was just about the only job they were allowed to have."

Emily read the section she had written about an unspeakable thing called the blood libel. "Believe it or not, there were people who thought that the Jews used the blood of Christian children for religious rituals. That's what 'The Prioress's Tale," by the famous poet Geoffrey Chaucer, is about." She read,

> The Jewish folk conspired
> Out of this world this innocent to chase;
> A murderer they found, and thereto hired,
> Who in an alley had a hiding-place;
> And as the child went by at sober pace,
> This cursed Jew did seize and hold him fast,
> And cut his throat, and in a pit him cast.

"Too much!" she heard Holly screech above gasps from the audience. Others shook their heads in disbelief.

"And if you think we've been having a raging epidemic here at Bromley with the German measles, the worst epidemic in history hit Europe in 1348," Emily continued. "The Bubonic Plague traveled on sailing ships from the East. Infected fleas bit rats and the rats passed the germs along to every country in Europe, thanks to poor sanitary conditions. The disease was so fatal that people dropped dead in the streets. Christians blamed the Black Death on the Jews. They accused them of poisoning the drinking water from the wells."

More gasps. Emily caught a look of horror on Old Foxy's face.

"I bet you never realized that 'Ring Around the Rosy,' the popular nursery rhyme, is about the rash of rose-colored circles that spread across the faces of Plague victims. 'A pocket full of posies' refers to the flowers that were used to get rid of putrid odors, and 'Ashes, ashes, all fall down' is about how people almost always died from the disease. To think that children still sing this today!"

It was Cressida's turn. "Around this time, something called the Inquisition started in Spain. Jews and Muslims were forced to convert to Christianity or they were imprisoned or put to death. But converting didn't really help. New Christians, or Conversos, as they were called, were suspected of practicing their old customs in secret and were burned at the stake. In 1492, the same year King Ferdinand and Queen Isabella sent Christopher Columbus on his voyage to the New World, they signed an edict ordering all Jews who hadn't converted to Christianity to leave Spain."

Emily read the next section. "It's because of the Inquisition that the first Jews made their way to New York, by a roundabout route through South America. The Inquisition went on for more than three centuries. Finally, the last heretic was burned at the stake in 1834."

She peeked at the audience again. She spied, in the corner of the assembly hall, a stout figure with flyaway orange hair wearing a white nurse's uniform with a muskrat coat draped over her shoulders. Then, in the blink of an eye, the figure was gone.

Cressida took over. "You'd think that would have been the end of it, but, as you know, less than fifteen years ago, we had World War II, when Adolf Hitler and the Nazis tried to conquer most of Europe. Some of our fathers fought in that war. Some, like Lindsley McGovern's father, were wounded or killed. Hitler blamed Germany's problems on the Jews and sent millions of them and others who disagreed with his policies to concentration camps, where most of them perished."

All right, so they went beyond the Middle Ages. The audience didn't look a bit bored and Miss Lockwood and Old Foxy didn't seem to mind.

It was Emily who had the last word. She had come to the part she hadn't written down. She took off her glasses. "Prejudice is a disease that poisons every period in history. We must fight that plague wherever it rears its ugly head, even here at Bromley." She squinted at the audience. "This year, in one grade, there was a club that ostracized the Jewish girls. And you all know about the posture pictures that are taken every fall and kept secret. Well, this time, a student happened to find them. Each picture had racial remarks on the bottom, attributing different body types to people from certain backgrounds. These labels had nothing to do with correcting curvature of the spine."

She could get expelled for this, Emily realized. But she'd finally done it. She'd spoken up loud and clear. Cressida stared at her with panic. "Don't worry," Emily whispered. "I won't tell who the members were."

Then a soft, low rumble, almost a hum, as in a theater before a show, could be heard from the audience. At first, Emily couldn't make out the words, or even if there were words. But soon it grew into a rhythmic chant: "Down with posture pictures! Down with prejudice!" First Emily's class, then the teachers, then the entire audience rose to its feet, clapping thunderously. If this were a quiz show, the applause meter would have shot up to one hundred, Emily thought.

She and Cressida made way for Miss Foxworthy, who walked up to the podium, extending her arms in a hushing motion. "I think you will all agree that we owe a debt of gratitude to Emily Winter and Cressida Whitcroft. Their presentation was quite exemplary. Perhaps some changes could be made, but that's for another assembly."

Miss Lockwood tried to have the girls exit in the usual orderly manner, but it was impossible. Everyone rushed up to Emily and Cressida, shouting congratulations.

"Amazing!"

"Incredible!"

"Brilliant!"

The compliments flew. Emily was a hero! I'm also a leader, she thought.

"I always thought there was something extra spooky about those posture pictures!" Lindsley said.

"What a great movie that Inquisition story would make!" Holly said. "James Dean would have been perfect as a pretend Christian burned at the stake!"

"Paul Newman can do it instead. Isn't he Jewish?" Margery said.

"There should be a piece to accompany this work, a fugue," Mr. Carslake said. "A variation on Gregorian chant, perhaps, a descant of mournful Middle Eastern tonalities—something like this." He hummed a dirge-like melody.

"Oh, Al—And you're the one to compose it!" Miss Lockwood cooed.

"I'll have a go at it over vacation," Mr. Carslake cooed back.

Even Miss Heath congratulated Emily. "Well done, Winter, I have to admit. Couldn't you have found an article on this topic for your cause assignment? You might have avoided that Passing Plus, which brought your semester average down to a Fair. In view of your paper, though, I might consider raising your grade to a Good Minus."

Emily couldn't have cared less. She had gotten her term paper grade earlier that morning.

Distinguished!

The sixth in Bromley's history. It didn't have a nickname, so Emily called it "Stingo," which caught on instantly.

"Who got the other two Stingos?" Emily's father asked.

Of course, Emily had to share her Stingo with Cressida. Once again, she felt a pang of sympathy. Cressida's mother wasn't there. She and her new husband were on their honeymoon.

There was another person who took some of the credit. "I did the typing," Emily's mother said.

Emily heard a familiar deep voice behind her.

"That was a remarkable piece of scholarship and writing, despite, I should point out, a few mixed metaphors," Davy said. "I was cognizant of many of the incidents, being familiar with most of your sources, but there was some fresh material, too."

Alice had invited him. They had what she called a "plaphonic" relationship, conducted by telephone because they lived too far away from each other. But finally Davy had taken the big step of traveling to Manhattan by himself. And Alice would be taking the train to Great Woods on Saturday. "I can't wait to see what a Long Island suburb is like!" she told Emily.

But Emily had her mind on something else. A boy with a scar had broken away from the mass of green jackets.

"Fantastic! Great job of research and writing! Even Ted here, a harsh critic, is impressed!" Rob said. He pushed a lock of hair, shaped like a teardrop, away from his eyebrows. She didn't mind that they met over his nose.

Ted popped up behind him. "Top drawer scholarship! Bravo! Couldn't have done better myself! You lifted the veil off some truly despicable events. And you had the courage to point out that prejudice against the People of the Book isn't a thing of the past. Those posture pictures will be banned, I'm sure."

"Thank you," Emily muttered. It was obvious that Rob and Ted thought of her as a grind—one of those frighteningly studious Bromley grade-grubbers with their noses always pressed into a book, who piled up top grades the way more fun loving girls collected headbands.

If that description applied to her, it applied to Cressida

too, didn't it? Maybe Emily could say, "Oh, most of the praise should go to Cressida!" But that might defeat the purpose. Rob would go over and congratulate her and probably fall in love with her.

The Kensington teacher, a stern-looking man with a gleaming, hairless dome, motioned for Rob and Ted to line up with the other boys.

"Who's that?" Lady Lenore asked, pointing to Rob as she wiped away tears with a monogrammed handkerchief.

"Just someone I know from Flora Freund's," Emily said.

27 ❀ A Hospital Gown

Cressida was standing at the foot of Phoebe's bed when Emily arrived.

"Why are you here?" she asked.

"Same reason you are. I'm Phoebe's friend, too," Emily said.

The nurse said Phoebe had been drifting in and out of sleep. She looked like a rag doll, in her baggy hospital gown with one arm hooked up to an IV pole. Her face was the same sallow shade as the green walls of her room. She reminded Emily of the people with matchstick arms and legs and squares for torsos she used to draw in kindergarten.

"Phoebe really came close to dying," Cressida said. "I guess Miss Heath should have given you a Stingo on your cause assignment, too, because she definitely had anorexia nervosa, or whatever it's called."

Grades, always grades. Still, Emily thought it was an incredible thing for Cressida to say.

Phoebe opened her eyes and turned her head slowly from side to side. "Cress . . . Em," she said weakly.

"Welcome back to the living!" Cressida said. She squeezed Phoebe's right hand. Emily squeezed her left.

Maybe it was like an algebra equation—if $x = y$ and $y = 2$, then $x = 2$. If Emily was a friend of Phoebe's and Cressida was a friend of Phoebe's, did Cressida + Emily = friends, too? Maybe she would even miss her when she was at boarding school next year, but that was probably going too far.

"It was really scary, Pheebs. Do you remember what happened?" Cressida asked.

"The flash from the camera," she said slowly. "Then polka dots and cobwebby patterns like a kaleidoscope. Everything spinning. That's when I must've passed out."

Cressida told how Mr. Lambroza had gone ahead with the yearbook picture, even with the school in an uproar. "And by the time he took it, my meeting with Miss Lockwood was over, and I could be in the picture, holding Eeyore," she said.

You didn't deserve to be in the picture, Emily was tempted to say. Especially in the most important position, smack in the middle of the front row.

Phoebe had a roommate: a girl named Linda, who had just had her tonsils out. Linda moaned a lot and regurgitated gobs of blood into a bedpan. It was because of the anesthetic. Ether made you sick to your stomach. Its faint, nauseating smell hung in the air. The nurse brought Linda a chocolate and vanilla Dixie cup but once again she was reaching for the bedpan.

"If she doesn't want her ice cream, maybe Phoebe will try it," Emily suggested.

The nurse rushed over. "Of course, dear child, but do eat slowly." She wore a white cardigan with one button fastened at the top, which fell over her shoulders like a cape. Pinned to her uniform, a nameplate read "Maureen."

Emily watched in awe as Phoebe dug in with the wooden spoon and scooped up a bit of chocolate ice cream. Then she tried the vanilla—just a speck, but still it was something. She probably hadn't tasted anything sweet in months.

It was five o'clock, suppertime for the patients, and carts were being wheeled to the rooms.

"Maybe Phoebe would like some dinner, too," Cressida said.

Maureen placed a plate of macaroni and cheese on the tray attached to Phoebe's bed.

After a mouthful, Phoebe said she was full. She sank back into her pillow.

"That's all right," Maureen said. "You have to go easy with the food at first."

A tall, gangly man in a lumber jacket and khakis brushed past Maureen and stopped at Phoebe's bedside. He set a vase of red roses on the night table.

"I'm here to take her home, Dr. Sturges," the man said as a woman with a white jacket and stethoscope came up behind him.

"I'm afraid we can't let her go just yet, Mr. Barrett," Dr. Sturges said. "She has just begun taking in some solid food. She could be doing it just to get out of here. We have to monitor her for a few days to make sure she isn't faking."

The man stared down at his beat-up, yellowing Keds. Emily recognized him; he was the striking, craggy-featured man in the photograph next to cousin Millie's on the dresser in Phoebe's room.

"My daughter wouldn't fake it. She's the most genuine person I know," he said.

Phoebe's eyes flew open. "That man sounds so much like my father," she said.

"He is your father," Cressida said.

Mr. Barrett leaned over and gave Phoebe an awkward hug.

"Daddy!" Tears spilled down Phoebe's haggard cheeks.

Emily couldn't help noticing that she didn't call him Bryce.

"Yes, Phoebe, I'm home. I've been here every day, ever since word reached me about your condition. There are no telephone lines in the bird sanctuary, but Mummy was able to get a telegram through to the nearest Western Union office. But this is the first time you've been conscious. I'd almost given up hope."

He called Mrs. Barrett Mummy, Emily noticed, and she suspected that's what Phoebe usually called her mother, too.

He looked at Cressida, then at Emily. "Girls, I know when Phoebe gets home, you'll help her get some meat on those bones."

"Don't worry, Mr. Barrett," Cressida said. "When she's back at school we'll make sure she eats nothing but fattening food, won't we?"

"Does she like pizza pie?" Dr. Sturges asked. "My patients tell me there's a place on Eighty-sixth Street that's quite popular."

"She used to love the pizza at Sal's!" Emily said.

Cressida pointed to Emily. "Mr. Barrett, have you met Emily Winter?"

Phoebe's father extended a calloused hand. "I've heard such good things about you, Emily."

"Daddy, these girls deserve a special award for saving my life," Phoebe said. "They called the ambulance when I fainted at school."

Emily had been the one to call the ambulance, but it would be too much to expect Cressida to refuse to share the credit.

"Girls, how can I ever thank you?" Phoebe's father said.

A worried look clouded Phoebe's face. "But, Daddy, are you home for good?"

"Yes, Phoebe, and not only that, I just accepted a position at Bromley. I'll be teaching a class on the natural sciences to the twelfth grade."

"Yay-ay-ay!" Phoebe cheered. Her voice was beginning to sound stronger.

"Now Mr. Carslake won't be the only man at Bromley!" Cressida said.

Emily wondered if Phoebe's mother would stop working at Best & Co., now that her father had a job.

Phoebe moved to the edge of the bed and lowered her feet to the floor. She put on a pair of paper slippers, which seemed to have been waiting for just this moment. She took some steps toward her father.

"Dr. Sturges, look at Phoebe!" Emily said.

"She is getting better," Dr. Sturges said. "But we can't discharge her just yet. And once she's home, she should drink a malted milk every day. She can't go back to school until she gains at least 10 pounds and she'll have to weigh in at my office once a week until she gets up to 112."

That was exactly what Phoebe's mother weighed, Emily couldn't help thinking.

"While you were, um, asleep, you got to miss a Special Assembly!" Cressida said. "For our term paper, Emily and I had to give a joint presentation about, you won't believe it, Jews in the Middle Ages."

Phoebe's eyes widened.

"How they were discriminated against and sometimes murdered," Emily said.

"We started with the Crusades," said Cressida. "Of course, Muslims were persecuted, too."

"You and Emily gave a presentation together?" Phoebe asked.

"Yes, and Emily talked about the captions on the posture pictures, but don't worry, she didn't mention your name."

"And we got a Distinguished, which we nicknamed Stingo," Emily said.

Phoebe looked terrified. "I never wrote my term paper! I never even got to choose a subject."

"Being in the hospital is an acceptable excuse, even at Bromley. I'm sure you'll be granted an extension," Emily said.

"We have another assignment," Cressida said. "The whole grade is going to see *The Diary of Anne Frank*. And now you'll be able to go!"

"It's so good! I can't wait to see it again," Phoebe said.

"You saw it?" Cressida said.

"Yes, on Emily's birthday."

"But——"

"I guess I didn't obey all the League rules," Phoebe said.

28 ❀ A Gift

"Good morning, Bromley girls!" Miss Lockwood said, standing in front of her desk. It was the last homeroom period before spring vacation.

"Good morning, Miss Lockwood!" The class chorused.

"Before we go over some class business, I have, as it were, some news." She pulled her left hand from where she had jammed it inside her suit jacket pocket and wiggled her fingers. On the fourth finger, a tiny round diamond twinkled.

"I have been given, as it were, a token of affection, a gift, to announce the fact that Mr. Carslake and I will be celebrating our nuptials over summer vacation."

"You mean, you're engaged?" Margery said.

"I knew it! I knew it!" Alice said.

"Quickly, someone put 'nuptials' in the Nifties!" Holly said.

"Oh, lordy, who doesn't know what that means?" Cressida groaned.

"Are you still going to teach at Bromley?"

"Can we come to the wedding?"

"Where will you go on your honeymoon?"

The questions were still flying as Mr. Carslake walked in with his mandolin. Someone started chanting, "Alex and Katie sitting in a tree." The others chimed in with "K-i-s-s-i-n-g."

Miss Lockwood's cheeks turned bubble-gum pink.

"So now can we hear an *aubade*?" Alice begged.

"How about one by Shakespeare? Surely, Juliet's words pass the Legion of Decency," Mr. Carslake said with a wink.

193

He strummed as he sang,

> Wilt thou be gone? it is not yet near day:
> It was the nightingale and not the lark,
> That pierced the fearful hollow of thine ear . . .

"You mean, Romeo and Juliet went all the way?" Margery asked.

"Maybe they were just making out all night," Holly said.

A group of girls had paused at the homeroom door. They were students who had been admitted for the following year and were touring Bromley again before making a final decision.

Emily thought of her own visit to Bromley last spring. She'd been in a bad mood. She hadn't wanted to move to New York, change schools, or have a baby sister or brother. Now she was happy about the first two things and more or less resigned to the third.

"Homerooms are the soul of the school," said Pamela Prescott, the tour leader.

There was a Negro girl in the group. She would probably be the only one in the school. The one Negro student at Bromley now was graduating this June. Emily knew that the new girl was Phoebe's neighbor, Dorothy. How would her classmates treat her? Emily promised herself she would keep an eye out for Dorothy in the fall.

"Yeah, homeroom period is when important announcements are made—such as when a favorite teacher gets engaged," Lindsley squealed. "Congrats to you, Miss Lockwood!"

The prospective students cheered, too.

School was dismissed after homeroom. "Come on over. Nobody's home, not even Louisa," Alice told Emily and Phoebe. "My parents went to Wellesley with Bettina to make sure that's where she wants to go. She got into Smith and Mount Holyoke, too."

In the courtyard at 1163 Park Avenue, daffodils were blooming. Vince doffed his hat. "You girls are a breath of sunshine!"

At Alice's, they flopped down on Bettina's twin beds.

"Miss Too-Perfect-For-Words!" Emily said. "And her boyfriend is Mr. Perfect, too!"

"Hmm," Alice muttered.

"Speaking of boyfriends, isn't that great about Miss Lockwood?" Emily said.

"Yeah, not too many Bromley teachers get married," Phoebe said. "I mean, there's no hope for Miss Stillman!"

"What about Miss Heath? She's an old maid if there ever was one!" said Alice. "Can you imagine her French kissing with those rotting teeth?"

"Or wearing a sheer negligee on her wedding night?" Emily said, collapsing in giggles on the flower-print carpet in Bettina's room.

She walked over to the dresser and idly picked up a silver hairbrush. It reminded her of a more masculine version Evan had received as a gift when he was born. She resisted the urge to take it. She hadn't stolen anything since the marble heart from Best & Co.

Her eyes strayed to the mirror above the dresser. Wedged into the frame were an invitation to an Easter cotillion at the Plaza Hotel, a notice about spring semester schedule changes at Bromley, which Emily had also received, and several doctors' appointment cards.

Bettina went to an orthodontist, Emily noted with surprise as she looked at the card signaling an April 11 appointment with Dr. Henry Popkin, who was also Alice's orthodontist. Bettina didn't wear braces and her teeth looked as perfect as the rest of her but maybe she needed one of those nighttime retainers.

Partially obscured by a wallet-sized picture of James Dean was another appointment card. "March 10, 9:30 a.m., Dr. Jorge Perez, Clínica San Juan Capistrano." That was the weekend Bettina and her parents had gone to Puerto Rico. But "clínica" didn't sound like a resort. Had she taken ill and gone to the hospital? That would explain why she'd come home without even a trace of a tan.

That's when it all clicked. Suzy in *Modern Romances*, who

couldn't afford to go to Puerto Rico. She had to sit out her pregnancy in an unwed mothers' home before putting up the baby for adoption.

Bettina, of course, could afford to go to Puerto Rico. Kit Chadwick had gotten her pregnant; Emily was quite sure of it. She could end her pregnancy; she could get rid of the baby. She could check into a clinic with real doctors and clean sheets.

Alice caught her looking at the appointment card. She snatched it and tore it up. She stuffed the shreds in her pocket.

"None of your beeswax, nosybody!"

"Did Bettina have an abortion?" Emily asked.

"What if she did?"

"Well, did she?"

"You didn't really expect her to have a baby out of wedlock like those girls in *Modern Romances,* did you?"

"So Bettina isn't Miss Perfect!"

"I guess not. I even feel a little sorry for her because she might not be able to go to Wellesley, after all. My parents say they want her to stay in town where they can keep an eye on her. She just applied to Barnard."

"Isn't it too late?" Emily asked. Anyway, being at home hadn't kept Bettina from getting into trouble, Emily couldn't help thinking.

"A recommendation from Old Foxy should be enough," Alice said. "It wasn't really Bettina's fault, you know. Kit was irresponsible—he should have used one of those prophylactics—you know, a rubber. And now that she's not a virgin, she might have trouble finding someone to marry her."

That's what people said, but Emily didn't believe it. "I'm sure she'll find a husband," she said.

Alice frowned. "I don't have to tell you not to breathe a word of this! Not a single syllable! Lips glued! Cross your heart and hope to die!"

29 ❀ Neckties

Staking out a table on the ground floor, Emily, Alice, and Phoebe had just started on their pizza and cherry Cokes when Cressida, Lindsley, Margery, Eugenia, and Holly trooped in. They sat down at the next table.

"I have a little thank you gift," Phoebe whispered. She leaned over and pressed a tissue-wrapped object into Emily's hand. It felt hard and smooth. She traced the unmistakable shape. A marble heart!

Emily had been feeling strangely hopeful all morning. Looking in the mirror, she hadn't found Cressida or Carol Lynley or the spitting image of her father, but herself—Emily Judith Winter, a Jewish girl with rippling black curls and an unusual brown fleck in one of her blue eyes.

A girl who had just gotten a Stingo. A Bromley girl.

In the elevator, she had remained calm when Cameron the Conceited got on. He raked his fingers through his hair.

"Hiya," he said, looking her in the eye.

"Hiya," she said, looking him in the eye, too.

"Great paper!" he said. "The one on the Middle Ages, I mean."

So he had been there, too! She bowed her head, then raised it again. There was no reason to feel intimidated. Cameron hadn't mentioned a single baseball score by the time they reached the lobby. If Emily hadn't been waiting for Alice, she might have walked out with him.

❀   ❀   ❀

Holly glanced over at Emily's table, then at Cressida. "I'm mixed up. Are we allowed to be friends with the Clothes Girls now?"

"You are so out to lunch!" Cressida said. "Don't you know there are no more Clothes Girls?"

"So there's no more League?"

Did Emily detect a faint look of regret on Cressida's face?

"There's still an ACGL—but now it stands for the Anti–Chatham Girls League," Lindsley explained. "We're snubbing Chatham because they don't have any Jewish students. Get it?"

"Kind of," Holly said.

"Praise the lord!" Cressida said.

"You'll never believe what I just did," Phoebe said.

"Gorged on a double banana split?" Alice ventured. She wasn't being sarcastic; Phoebe had been feasting on high-calorie desserts ever since she left the hospital. In fact, she was even getting a little chubby, but Emily had made Alice promise not to say anything

"Nope, not even warm. Last night I packed up all Cousin Millie's clothes to donate to the Bromley-Chatham Exchange. It took some doing, but Mummy finally agreed to get rid of them. Who wants to wear a dead debutante's gowns? Especially one who died the way she did."

"That terrible horse-jumping accident," Emily said.

"That's the official story," Phoebe said. "She botched the jump but she wasn't badly hurt. But losing was too humiliating. That night, she swallowed a whole bottle of sleeping pills."

Cressida gasped. "She killed herself because she didn't win?" There was something not quite convincing about her dismay, Emily thought, as if she might have had similar dark ideas herself.

"That's like committing suicide if you get a Fair Minus," Alice said.

Phoebe's cousin had gone to boarding school, but she was probably like many of the girls at Bromley, Emily thought.

Like Cressida. The strain of living up to her reputation had become too much for her. Eventually flaws seeped through the fragile veneer, like the snow through Phoebe's leaky galoshes.

Emily watched as Sal slapped and stretched a filmy sheet of pizza dough with his fists and tossed it in the air. For a split second, it hung there, bobbing gracefully. Emily found herself wishing she could float on top of it.

"Look who's here!" Alice said just as Rob and Ted strutted through the door. They loosened their ties and slung them over their shoulders the way Kensington boys always did as soon as school let out.

Emily whipped off her glasses. She didn't want to float away anymore. She wanted to stay right where she was, here in New York City, in the year 1956. If only everyone would just freeze, like in a game of Statues: Sal tossing pizza dough in the air, Rob fidgeting with his tie, Alice slurping her cherry Coke.

But the dough landed and turned into crusty pizza, Rob took off his tie, and Alice ordered another cherry Coke.

Everything was in constant motion, everything was always changing, and so was Emily. And some day, years from now, Sal's might be gone, along with the Peachtree, the Automat, and 1163 Park Avenue.

But not Bromley. Emily had a feeling it would last forever.

"I know I'm repeating myself, but that was a fine presentation," Rob said, pulling up a chair next to Emily's. Cressida's mouth fell open. Alice pinched Emily's thigh.

"If I may say so, I couldn't have done better myself," said Ted.

Emily wished they would just drop the whole thing. "Thank you," she said half-heartedly.

Ted squeezed in next to Cressida. "I would adore nothing more than to attend future Bromley assemblies, but it's adieu and *arrivederci* to Kensington for yours truly. I'll be in Connecticut at Hotchkiss next year, leaving the Robber here to fend for himself."

"Me too! I'm going to boarding school next year," Cressida trilled. "Amber Hill. It's in Connecticut, too."

Emily wondered if Ted had heard of Amber Hill. She thought she caught a glimmer of surprise on his face.

"Guess who's coming back next year!" Phoebe said. "Juliet Dunne. Her parents' divorce came through and she and her mother don't have to live in Nevada anymore. You'll just love her, Emily, and you, too, Alice. I know you will!"

Emily wasn't so sure, even though there was no reason they couldn't all be friends. And maybe, after a year at Amber Hill, Cressida's problems would be cured and she'd come back to Bromley.

The pizza was ready. Sal set the pan on the table. Emily offered Rob a slice.

"Gosh, thanks. You're sure you don't want it?" Folding it in half, he aimed the pointy end at his mouth and wolfed it down.

"Who's that?" Lindsley asked.

"Emily's boyfriend," Phoebe said matter-of-factly.

Boyfriend—that was a nifty word!

"They're going together," Phoebe added.

She was a true friend, Emily thought. "Friend"—the niftiest word of all.

"Where do you live?' Rob asked Emily.

"1163 Park."

"The building that looks like a castle? The one with a driveway that's like a moat?"

Everyone said her building looked like a castle, but she had never heard anyone else compare the driveway to a moat before. "That's the one."

I'll walk you home," Rob said.

The butterflies in Emily's stomach were doing cartwheels. What would they talk about? Would it be like her cousin Gordon's bar mitzvah party last year? He lived in Philadelphia. Emily hadn't known any of the eighth and ninth graders at her table. She'd kept trying to join the conversation but it was like trying to carve a path through people waiting in line who refused to let you by.

"I think I heard that next year the Kensington and Bromley upper schools will have woodworking together," Rob said.

"At Bromley or at Kensington?" Emily asked. Was this what they were going to talk about?

"I think we'll probably alternate—one week at Bromley, the next at Kensington."

Of course. How else would they do it? Woodworking would probably be Emily's worst subject, a guaranteed Fair Minus, and how could she build furniture without wearing her glasses?

Emily stared at the red light on the corner of Park and Ninetieth. Would it ever turn green?

Rob offered her a stick of Juicy Fruit. She unwrapped it and popped it in her mouth. They chewed in silence.

Rob spit his gum into a corner trashcan. "I don't suppose you've seen this new movie *Tea and Sympathy*? he asked. "It's at the Trans Lux. I think there's a two o'clock show on Saturday. Want to go?"

How could she tell him she'd rather see *Rebel Without a Cause*? Surely he'd already seen it. *Tea and Sympathy* was about a shy new student at a boys' boarding school who has an affair with the headmaster's wife. There were sure to be love scenes. Emily always squirmed when couples kissed on-screen, and the lead in *Tea and Sympathy* was John Kerr, a dreamy Harvard graduate.

That's when it dawned on her that she hadn't looked at the creased poster of Laurence Olivier since Fräulein had caught her practice-kissing. It had stayed rolled up on her closet shelf for months.

"Yes," Emily heard herself say, "I'd like to go." She would probably never get to see *Rebel Without a Cause*.

The light had changed and they walked past the banks of tulips that had begun to sprout on the narrow strips of concrete dividing Park Avenue.

Emily could feel Rob's eyes on her. "You know, I've owed you an apology for the longest time," he said. "For that idiotic practical joke at Froggy's, I mean Flora Freund's. It's kind of complicated but the reason I tricked you is because sometimes I feel the need to pretend I'm someone else. Usually I want to be Ted, who's Mr. Suave and doesn't have a hideous scar."

That's what Emily had imagined him saying, when she had sobbed into her pillow after the class dance.

"It's not hideous," she said. "It's interesting."

"You really think so?" Rob stared at her in amazement.

She nodded. "How did it happen?"

Emily was ready for a boring explanation. A drag-down fight with his brother—did he have a brother? Or a fall from a tree house, landing in sharp branches. Weren't boys always falling from tree houses? But maybe he had spent his entire life in New York City. Maybe he'd never even seen a tree house.

"In a jousting tournament," Rob said as they crossed the moat-like driveway to the building that looked like a castle.

Martha Mendelsohn has worked as a translator for the French Embassy, an editorial assistant for Holt, Rinehart and Winston, and associate editor of *Tikkun* magazine. Her fiction and non-fiction have appeared in *Tikkun*, *The New York Times*, *Moment*, *Beliefnet.com*, *Jewishmag.com*, and *The Jewish Week*. She lives with her husband on Manhattan's Upper West Side.